Beatrice Belongs To Me

CURSED FROM BIRTH

SAVANNA LOY

To the one person who drives me the craziest. Thank you for the push I needed to start this author journey. It wasn't a gentle push, it was a deep-dive right off the cliff, kinda push.

Which is exactly what it took. This is my true first book ever written, the secret project I've been afraid to share with the world. No turning back now. This book is solely dedicated to you, my annoyingly wonderful husband whom I have loved more than half my life.
Happy Birthday Jode, I love you.

Chapter 1: Tragic Beginnings

They say you can't be born evil. But what if your mother suffers from a severe mental health condition? What if her hobbies include manipulation, exploitation, violating others' rights, anger, arrogance, lying, stealing, animal abuse, and other colorful interests? With those genes coursing through your DNA, does it make a difference?

Christine Damion was perhaps one of the vilest women you could ever encounter. Something about her yellow-toothed, crooked smile could turn knots in your stomach. She reeked of cigarette smoke and cheap fur. Oddly enough, despite her many flaws, she had a knack for charming people, bending them to her will. She knew how to build people up, but what was more impressive—and more terrifying—was the way she could tear them down. It seemed she derived the most pleasure from being the puppet master, pulling the strings of those around her.

In a twist of fate, Ms. Damion's life was about to be forever changed.

News spread of her pregnancy and most thought this would finally be the answer to the personality make-over that she desperately needed. Nobody could have foreseen how she would really feel, although looking back, nobody should have been surprised. After her explosive bouts of anger towards the idea of her body losing its skeletal shape, she devised the most sinister of plans. She decided that this new baby would be exactly what she needed to take her manipulation to the next level. She knew she could get anybody to do anything she wanted if she could use a baby as her ploy. With a new-found mission of manipulation, Ms. Damion took active measures to ensure a safe pregnancy.

Looking back, it's a relief that she wanted to use her offspring as bait in devious plans because if she hadn't seen a way to use the newborn as a meal ticket, who knows what she would have done to avoid delivery. On the other hand, if she would have found a way to terminate, the world would have never faced Christofer. Sadly, a world without Christofer Damion would have probably been the preferred choice.

The day had finally arrived. The drive to the hospital, where most mothers are usually riddled with a whirlwind of emotions, was different for Ms. Damion. For most, meeting their child for the first time is a moment of blissful adoration, immense relief, unexpected elation, and joy.

But Ms. Damion was not most mothers. She chose to drive herself to the hospital, a decision she viewed as bold and independent. She knew she could do this without help from anyone. Although she had contemplated several schemes to manipulate someone else into doing it for her, she always arrived at the same conclusion: her son would mark the beginning of one of the longest cons she could have ever dreamed of, and she was truly excited to meet him. To her, going to the hospital alone was a choice—her choice.

In reality, she had no one. Through a life of manipulating others and taking anything she wanted, she had completely alienated herself. There wasn't one soul left in the world that would willingly help or be there for her. Sure, she could con them, she was so good at twisting words.

If given the sober choice, no manipulation involved, there wasn't one person she would have been able to call on. As she screeched into the parking lot, she could feel the contractions getting closer. This child was strong, she could feel it. When most mothers would fantasize about their child's future as a football player, doctor, or lawyer; she was fantasizing about all the people's lives they would ruin together as they enjoyed the financial aftermath.

After getting signed in, she refused any assistance from the nursing staff to wheel her to her room. "I walked in here on my own two legs, I can go to my room on my own two legs, I'm no cripple," she arrogantly barked. As she waddled down the sterile hallway, her pain was intensifying. She knew this child was coming fast, and she was very pleased.

Finally making it to her empty room that buzzed with noises of machinery beeping, she nearly collapsed into the bed. She didn't want to admit it, but this was taking more out of her than anything had before. She yelled for nurses to hurry up and get her some assistance. After getting checked from the nursing staff, she lay in her stiff bed staring at the stark white ceiling tiles. She was literally counting down the minutes until her son was to be born. She was elated that this was the end to her annoying cramps, un-welcomed bloating, and aggressive heartburn. She didn't even seem fazed by the empty burgundy pleather chairs in the room where loved ones should be.

The lack of flowers or gifts for the expecting mother and newborn didn't seem to faze her either. Instead, she gleaned at the thoughts of the devious duo she and her child would become. It was time. She knew it and she contemplated just delivering the child herself, but the hospital wouldn't allow it. After several hours of intense pushing, the baby was here.

The delivery was very difficult, and the birth was painful. The doctors even hinted at how much of a fighter the infant was, and this brought on an odd sense of sick pride to the malevolent mother. It was finally done, the nurse handed that blue, cotton-swaddled bundle of love to his new mother. Ms. Damion lay there imagining every sick and twisted con she could do for the next 18 years. As soon as their eyes locked, the picturesque image that was portrayed came across to the nurses as the sweetest moment they had seen from such a harsh woman.

The nurses couldn't have predicted her next reaction and were genuinely shocked! She was filled with disgust and rage. She let out a blood curdling scream and demanded that the child be removed from her immediately. With shock and confusion, a nurse grabbed the now crying baby Christofer from the vehement mother and held him close. She couldn't wrap her head around the issue. She didn't have to wait long for the answer.

"Have you seen that thing, that monster?" she shrieked. "I could never use a child like that. I just wasted 10 months of my life harboring an alien. I don't want it, take it away this instance."

Her mind was made up; her maternal instinct was not to love her child unconditionally. This had never happened before, and the nurse wasn't sure what to do. She gently lay the baby down in the plastic baby bed and started wheeling him to the hospital nursery. "Go ahead and call the authorities while you're at it, so I can do what needs to be done," ordered Ms. Damion.

That evening she signed the necessary papers to make young Christofer a ward of the state. Within seconds of his entrance into the world, Christofer had already lost what most deem the most precious gift ever given: the love and bond of mother and child.

One can only go up from such a tragic start. Things had to turn around for this child. What could his mom have witnessed to promote such a reaction. It was never known.

Normally, proper procedure for a newborn turned over to the state is very positive. Usually the child is taken into custody, looked after at an orphanage, and a forever family adopts them. They then begin their new life, usually better off than they were before. There are many couples looking for a baby, so small Christofer should have had many options to find a home. This was not the case for him. It seemed as if every couple who interviewed to adopt him, decided against it. For some it was his odd features, but for most it was the bizarre disposition.

Baby Damion was most politely described as peculiar looking. His alabaster skin appeared a sick shade of gray next to his burnt orange hair. That was paired with a very petite frame. The normal developments of children were particularly difficult for him because his left arm was six inches shorter than his right. The most awkward element of his appearance was the ambrosia-colored birthmark centered on his fore-head. There was gossip that the birthmark was left on his fore-head because of how twisted his own mother's mind had been. Of course, most don't believe in those old omens, but it was the biggest mark anyone had seen and many speculations were made of how it came to be. His worst feature had to be his lifeless chestnut eyes. Even though they were very small in size, when you gazed into them, it was as if Christofer was staring right through you. His eyes were like looking into a void to another world.

As far as orphanages go, there were three options. The prized choice was Future Steps Orphanage. This was the most pristine of the three. With immaculate facilities and a long waiting list, children never stayed more than three weeks at this facility. It was incredible how many wonderful families were brought together due to the diligence of Future Steps. A close second in success rate was Blessed Assurance Orphanage. Although there was no waiting list, this was a very well-loved facility. The staff all worked as volunteers and you could really see the love they had for the children. Blessed Assurance was most known for its education program it developed for the children who lived on property. With a first-class education being offered and the love and care the staff provided, this was most definitely a safe haven for children. Most children were adopted within the first year of being placed here. Some of the teenagers who were placed to live here between the ages of 15-18, opted to stay at Blessed Assurance indefinitely as volunteers. Christofer would have been well taken care, loved, educated, and well on his way to a bright future with either of these choices. Nevertheless, the fates never had that in the cards for him. His placement was assigned to New Hope Orphanage. The last choice anyone would make.

It was a 30-minute drive from the police station to the orphanage. Newly hired Officer McDonald was assigned the duty of dropping off the infant at the orphanage. Eager to please, he didn't balk at the assignment. In his head, he knew it was basically a babysitting gig, but his whole life he had dreamed of being on the police force and was anxious to do anything.

As the police clerk went to get the child, Officer McDonald started wondering how someone could give up a child. He himself was only in his early 20's and wasn't ready for a family, but he knew one day he would love to be a dad. The idea of just signing away a child, like an unwanted package, angered him a little. This was one of the many reasons he wanted to join law enforcement. He wanted to do right by the wronged; he wanted to bring justice to those who had lost the chance. He wanted to make a positive difference in all those he met. The more he thought about it, the happier he was that he got this assignment. What a great way to start, doing exactly what he wanted to, changing a life.

As Daisy turned the corner with a very tattered and dirty car seat, McDonald almost yanked it out of her hand because of his excitement to help this child. "You can't take it without signing the proper paperwork," squeaked Daisy. Of course he knew this; he was just ready to get started. After filling out all the necessary documents he was ready to head off. When he finally turned the car seat around, he was startled by the child's appearance. He quickly looked past the odd features and was captivated by his eyes. At only three days old, his eyes had an eerie maturity about them that intrigued and intimated the enthusiastic officer. They stared at each other for only a few seconds, but it felt like time had stopped for Officer McDonald.

Surprisingly, Christofer Damion did something that he had

not yet done with anyone else. He appeared to smile. It was only a half-smile, but it was still a smile. This made the officer very happy and he even reached out and patted the baby on the head, much like you would a dog. There was no response to the touch, which was likely due to the lack of bonding the child received because of the rejection of his mother. Satisfied by this simple interaction, Officer McDonald and Christopher Damion headed off to make the delivery.

As they drove to New Hope, one could only wish that the officer would have given an iota of thought to the place he was delivering this small child. On the way to New Hope, you actually pass Blessed Assurance Orphanage. If Officer McDonald would have maybe given more thought to the actual placement and not just of completing the assignment, then maybe poor Christofer Damion would have been changed forever. The encounter with the officer and the car ride to the orphanage was perhaps the safest, nicest, and most positive environment that Christofer would experience until the age of four. Without him even knowing, this officer was one of only people who showed Christofer what a normal and even loving person could look like.

Once off the main road, to get to New Hope you must drive down a very long and beat-up road. Rotted Hawthorn trees lined the drive. Surely at one time these trees made a beautiful arbor, decorating the path. Now, they were reminiscent of a haunted canopy that illuminated the idea of death. The concrete mostly consisted of holes rather than solid concrete. It made for a most unpleasant drive. As the duo bumped down the long drive, the Officer kept thinking about how exciting it would be to fill out his first police report showing his completed assignment. He was elated that his first assignment was going so well. As he neared the building, he started feeling reservations. He had never been down the driveway, let alone in the building. He had heard city horror stories but chalked it up to over dramatic gossip. The stories did not do the place justice. It was worse than he had ever heard.

Putting the car in park, he debated even getting out of the car.

How could anyone even live here?

Based on the outer shell of what was supposedly a place of refuge, he knew deep down this was no place for a child. Christofer started whimpering in the background and he knew he had to make a choice. With the car in park, he sat and weighed the options. He never expected to have such a dilemma the first day on the job. He didn't want to be the newbie officer who questioned orders, sounded like a know-it-all, or seemed as if he could do his job better than his superiors. However, he knew in his heart, this was a terrible choice for any child, let alone one who already had it so tough. Staring at the building, he knew he couldn't do it. Dream job or not, this was a little boy's life. His hand was shaking as he grabbed the gear shift; he knew this could end his career before it really began. He shifted into reverse, eased off the brake, and looked into his rearview mirror to turn around. The sight of Ethel in his mirror made him jump in his seat and he nearly knocked his coffee over that was sitting in the cup holder in the center console.

Where did she come from and how did she get behind my squad car?

First day on the job and he nearly ran over one of the town's oldest living residents. As he put the car back in park and rolled down his window, Ethel approached the vehicle.

"You getting out of the car or what?" she accused.

He reluctantly opened the door and shook her icy hand.

"I don't have all day, there is lots to do in an orphanage," she complained.

"Sorry ma'am, I was just making sure I had the right place for this fellow," he explained.

"You do, now just set him on the porch and be on your way, I'll take it from here," she commanded.

Now feeling like he was backed in a corner, the new officer panicked. Just seconds before, he had decided not to leave the child, but now he didn't know what to do since his most awkward encounter with the caretaker.

He carefully unstrapped the car seat, refusing to even look at Christofer. With Ethel watching, he slowly walked towards the huge metal door to the orphanage. It had been gratified multiple times through the years. His heart wrenched inside. He set the car seat down, took a deep breath and stepped away.

"Please sign these acceptance forms ma'am," he quivered.

"Yeah, yeah, yeah, I know the drill," Ethel grumbled.

"Please take good care of him, will ya?" he almost begged.

"This ain't my first rodeo, cowboy," she mocked.

She handed him the forms back and pushed past him. The aroma of rotting animals filled his nostrils. It made him a bit queasy. He turned as she snatched the car seat up, opened that huge metal door, and disappeared inside. He stood for a few seconds, trying to convince himself that this was going to be ok, but he knew better. As he got back in his squad car, he doubted the justice system for the first time in his life. He once again put the car in reverse and turned to head towards the police station. Back down the bumpy driveway, he thought about that little half-smile and his heart ached. With one last look in the rear-view mirror, a lonely tear fell from his eye.

Chapter 2: New Hope

New Hope orphanage was anything but that. It was amazing the city health inspector hadn't shut the place down years before. There were three stories of rusted metal that made up the main structure. Walking up to the front door, you could almost feel the disappointment from past children who lived there and were never adopted.

There was a strong smell of cat urine that oozed from every room. The sole caretaker was a cat fanatic and allowed every city stray to inhabit the empty rooms of the orphanage. Everyone in town knew this was the orphanage you went to when all hope seemed lost for the chance of adoption. This is where you go to grow up alone without a family. A better suited name for this dump would have been No Hope orphanage.

This was the very next chapter in Christofer's life. As Ethel carried him down a very dim lit hallway, she didn't bother avoiding ramming his car seat into the walls. The interior walls had once been painted a beautiful butter color.

Twenty years ago, this orphanage was intended to be a place full of hope, dreams, and love. Fast-forward and now those same walls that were once intended to ignite a cherry disposition to all who saw them, had faded into a very chalky nauseating yellow. Paired with various shades of ink, marker, and crayon drawings, the walls alone showed the lack of care that had gone into the facilities as time progressed.

As Ethel turned the corner, she rammed the car seat so hard

into a wall, a bit of the sheet rock was damaged. Jolting the baby awake, he started whimpering.

"Oh, don't you start that now," she whined back.

It had been several years since she had a child to care for, which was probably for the best. She brought the child into the filthy kitchen and sat him on the table. There was about 4 oz. left in a bottle in his car seat. She grabbed the blanket that was covering him and used it to prop the bottle in his mouth, to quiet him. She took a deep breath, sat back in one of the mismatched metal chairs that surrounded the table, and wondered if after all these years, she could actually do this.

Ethel was once a well-groomed, sweet, and intelligent kindergarten teacher. She adored her children and loved the idea of helping to teach them the very foundation of skills required to begin their education journey. She really felt like if she could make a difference in each child's life, she would have been a success. At only 5'5, she was a very small girl, with an even smaller frame. Her gorgeous blonde hair flowed all the way down her back. She had fair skin, with a tint of rose to her cheeks and the most adorable freckles around her nose. Her emerald eyes were full of love and kindness.

Her favorite color had to be purple, she found a way to incorporate it into almost every outfit. She was truly beautiful inside and out. She never needed any make-up because her natural beauty was overwhelming. It was a no-brainer that she had caught the eye of Ryder.

He was the school's gym teacher and equally loved his job. He was average height with a head full of the thickest brown locks. He had a scruffy goatee that donned his chin. He too had kind eyes. His were a soft shade of brown, and you could just see the care in them. If only one flaw, he had the oddest shaped nose, which if ever was attempted to be portrayed, was never done quite the way it should have been.

The couple turned heads everywhere they went. They complimented each other so well. It wasn't love at first sight, but more like love after the first three dates. Ethel knew she had found her soul-mate. Ryder knew he had found his soul-mate.

For two years, they were inseparable. Ryder came from money. His family did very well in the oil industry and left Ryder with enough money to live well and never work another day in his life. He only worked because he truly enjoyed it. This was one of the qualities Ethel cherished about her beau. They had bold dreams for their future. They were going to make a difference in children's lives forever.

After two years of the perfect dating relationship, they both felt like they were ready for the next step. One very sunny summer day, Ryder took his love on a picnic.

"Oh Ryder, picnics are my favorite!" she squealed with delight.

"You are my favorite," he romantically replied.

Hand in hand they headed to a place she had never been. Beautiful Hawthorn trees had created an arbor along a dirt path that almost completely guarded them from the sun. As they continued down the path, Ryder's hands started to get sweaty.

"What's wrong?" questioned Ethel.

"Nothing, dove," he reassured, "just a hot day."

Satisfied with the answer, they stopped at the end of the Arbor. They were surrounded by an empty field covered in butterweed flowers. At that moment, looking around, Ethel felt the happiest she had ever been. She had the love of her life, an incredible job, and the prettiest setting she had ever seen. She was a lucky girl. The two began their picnic with laughter, inside jokes, and the sheer enjoyment of each other's company. When the meal was ending, and it seemed as if it was time to start heading back, Ryder insisted that Ethel close her eyes.

"Close my eyes?" she questioned.

"Hey, I just made you a lovely meal, the least you can do is humor me," Ryder teased.

"Fine, but you have ten seconds and then I'm peeking," Ethel prompted.

He only needed three seconds. He went behind one of the Hawthorns and grabbed a tiny animal carrier.

"Ok, open!" he exclaimed. Ethel adored animals and let out a squeal of excitement.

"You haven't even seen what's inside," he said. As he opened the door, a very timid calico kitten emerged. Ethel scooped it up in her arms, thrilled at the gift.

"Wait, you have to read its name tag, you're going to love what I picked," stuttered Ryder.

Attached to the cat's purple and diamond studded collar was a name tag, but it didn't have a name on it. Instead the tag simply said, say yes. Confused, Ethel looked up to question the bizarre name. When she did, she saw Ryder on one knee, with a gorgeous emerald ring that almost matched the shade of her eyes in his hand.

"Well, what do you say?" he questioned.

She of course said yes. The couple was elated. For Ethel, this day literally couldn't be more perfect. As they lay on their picnic blanket for hours, they talked about their future together. Their home, their children, and their dreams were all discussed under the shade of those Hawthorns. Sitting up promptly, Ryder was almost giddy.

"I got it! Let's build an orphanage right here on this land. Let's make sure we can always have a part in making children's lives better. We will paint the walls the same color as these butterweeds, so we can remember this very day," he gushed with excitement.

"We could be the new hope for these children who will so desperately need it," Ethel replied almost in tears.

The two agreed and began plans immediately. With Ryder's financial resources, he was able to hire contractors and the whole project only took one year to complete. They got married in the very spot they hatched their idea one year previous. Ethel, Ryder, and now two cats, Hawthorn and Butter, moved into their new home that same night. The new couple was unstoppable. They had everything approved for their new orphanage in only six months. They were going to change the world, one child at a time.

Death is a fickle thing. Nobody plans for it, yet it is the one thing that will derail everything you had planned for in life. Some handle it better than others. They take their normal amount of grieving time, find a way to cope, and move on with their life. They cherish the memories of their loved ones, but their life doesn't end, it's just different. This was not the case for poor Ethel. It was a very cold winter's night and Ethel and Ryder had just finished dinner in the orphanage. They lived on the third floor because they wanted to be the primary caretakers of the place to make sure any future children placed here would be properly taken care of.

She wanted ice cream. Ryder had given her such a hard time about it, wondering how in the world she could crave such an icy treat when it was 10 degrees outside. She knew he would get it for her, she was married to the sweetest guy in the world. As predicted, he offered to run up the road and grab her as much ice cream as her heart desired. It was only 8:30, he joked he would still be back in time to watch their favorite show together. Ethel and her cats snuggled on the couch, while Ryder prepared to leave. As she kissed her love, she had no idea that was the last time their lips would meet.

"I love you, love," she cooed.

"I love you, dove," he replied.

He left their living room and walked down the stairs, for the last time. She was content, her life was perfect. She grabbed a blanket, snuggled deeper into the couch with Hawthorn and Butter thinking about how good her life was, while she was waiting for her love to return, and of course her chocolate ice cream.

The doorbell jolted Ethel awake. She had fallen asleep on the couch and didn't realize it. Looking at her watch, she couldn't believe it was already 10:30.

"Ryder," she called out, "someone is at the door."

The doorbell rang again.

"Ryder, can you get that?" she groaned.

This time the doorbell was pushed three times in a row. She assumed he had come home, saw her asleep, and didn't have the heart to wake her. As she got off the couch to answer the door, she was excited to get back upstairs for her ice cream. She had no idea who could be at the door this late, maybe it was their first child coming to the orphanage.

"I got it, love," she hollered, assuming Ryder must be in the bathroom. As she made her way down the stairs to the door, she could feel the icy chill from the harsh winter outside.

She reluctantly opened the door and to her surprise saw two officers standing there. Their brief conversation was a blur as the pain and shock of what they were telling her engulfed her. How could this happen, he was just going right down the road? Why did he swerve? Why didn't he just hit that stupid dog? Noble Ryder had swerved to miss a stray dog and hit a patch of ice on the road. When officers arrived on scene, they saw the overturned vehicle. It was still running, the heat, radio, and lights were all still going. When they approached the vehicle, it was an unforgettable sight. Glass, blood, and melted chocolate ice cream were everywhere. There was nothing they could do; Ryder was dead on arrival. She couldn't stomach what they were saying and vomited right there on her doorstep. Why did she send him to get ice cream? Because of her, her one true love was now dead.

Deterioration is a funny thing. It has applications to personalities, health, and buildings. It's a very negative word, and its exact antonym is improvement. After the accident, both Ethel and New Hope did exactly that; they deteriorated. It was a very slow and painful process. Ethel basically gave up on life. She changed everything. After the dust had settled from the funeral, Ethel inherited all of Ryder's money. She was his soul heir. That is because she was his soul mate. She never loved him for his money, that was the last thing she cared about. She would have moved to a remote island with no resources if she was able to go with Ryder. She loved all the things in her life, but Ryder was the heartbeat that made it all worthwhile.

It is better to have loved and lost, than to never love at all. She did not agree with that. Where her heart once was, she now felt a dark and painful hole. Life was literally too much to bear. With all that inherited money, she quit her job. She had enough to live two lives worth and still not ever need anything. Now with no job, she had plenty of free time to wallow in her despair. She couldn't even stand to look at herself in the mirror. When she did, she was reminded of all the nice things he had to say about her beauty.

She guessed that explained her drastic change in appearance. She chopped all her hair off and dyed it fire engine red. Her once long, shiny blonde locks, hung right near her chin. She also took to wearing make-up. The way she did it though looked more like she was auditioning to be a rodeo clown. She always loved purple, but now expressed that love by surrounding her entire eyes with it. She gave up on fashion and usually put on her favorite nightgown that was blood red in color. She used that as inspiration and painted her lips the exact same shade. She hardly ever wore shoes, instead she made slippers her choice of footwear. She looked unkempt and manic. She didn't care. She was literally trying to make herself as ugly on the outside as she felt on the inside.

She did no better by the orphanage. Several had questioned why she wouldn't just sell the thing and get a fresh start. She always snapped at this question. How dare they try to encourage her to sell the last thing she had left of Ryder. This was their future, and oddly enough, just being in its four walls gave her the sense he was still with her. She couldn't imagine ever leaving it. She never did. If she needed anything, she just called a service and had it delivered. She wouldn't even allow them to enter the building, they were told to drop it at the door and be on their way. She never wanted contact with the outside world. The strays were different though. Any cat without a place to go was welcome to come and go as they pleased. New Hope became the place of the crazy cat lady indeed.

It didn't take much for the orphanage to fall apart. Once you stop cleaning and fixing things that break, you are left with a building that should have been condemned. It was amazing to the town that children were even placed there. It was even more shocking that Ethel took them in. She felt she had a duty to try and at least carry on part of Ryder's dream. She would take in children who nobody else wanted. She would only do it for a short period of time. It was like as soon as they checked in, she started a clock. She would allow a child to be at the orphanage for exactly two years. Once two years hit, to the day, early in the morning she would phone the authorities to come and get them. Two years is how long Ethel and Ryder dated before he proposed. Maybe for her, any longer than two years would be too much, and she couldn't commit to keeping them in her life longer than that. Maybe in her own way she was protecting herself, afraid to lose anyone else she allowed into her life. Whatever the reason, she made no exceptions.

She was not a very good care-taker of either the children or the building. It was nothing for dirty dishes to be stacked in the sink, cat urine and feces to be everywhere, and trash to be piled up for days. The children were required to do all the maintenance and cleaning around the orphanage. Ethel only came down from the third floor three times a day. It was always a mystery to what she did up there. She had very little contact with the children, which was her safeguard. Unfortunately, children left to themselves is bad for them and the building. With limited rules, the children did as they pleased. They colored on the walls and put holes in things. They were not made to take regular baths or do any of their studies. The only thing Ethel made sure of was that they were fed three times a day. She would come down from the third floor, cook for the children, and they would all eat together. As soon as they were finished, she would push herself from the table, and leave. She never even spoke to them; she just sat there and ate with them. It was a very sad and lonely life for all who entered New Hope Orphanage.

The day that Officer McDonald brought Christofer to the orphanage, was a very difficult day for Ethel. It was her anniversary. She heard the car pulling into the driveway. When she went to the window and saw the squad car sitting in her driveway, she tried to remember the last time anyone had brought her a child. She didn't want to do this anymore. She just wanted to be left alone to die. She decided she wasn't even going to answer the door. He would get the hint and leave. After all, she wasn't the only orphanage in town. As she was closing the curtain, she saw it. A car seat in the back of the car. They were bringing her a baby! Whose bright idea was it to send a baby to her. She didn't take in babies! She felt an odd sensation in her body. Her heart skipped a beat. She felt a little bit of warmth inside her, that she hadn't felt in twenty years. It was a strange and distant feeling, and she didn't know what she thought about it. Her curiosity got the best of her, she had to go down there and see what this was all about. She slinked down the stairs, taking quicker steps with each stair. She almost felt excited, well as excited as she could get anymore. When she got outside, the officer still hadn't exited the vehicle. She wondered what he was doing. She wanted to get a closer look at the car seat, so she went around to the back of the vehicle. As she approached the rear of the vehicle, she peered into the back window to look at the child. Suddenly, the vehicle started moving backwards.

What kind of idiot cops was the city hiring with her tax dollars?

If she had enough energy she would sue the city for attempted manslaughter.

She was at least going to give him a piece of her mind. She approached the window of the vehicle, as he rolled the window down. The look on his face stopped her dead in her tracks. She had quickly rehearsed some very hateful things she was going to say, but it all faded. Instead she demanded he take the child to the door and then be on his way. She brought the child in and took him to the kitchen.

Now as she sat there looking at him, she was ready for the challenge. All the other children they had brought to her were already so old and set in their ways. This was different. This was her chance to teach this child how the world really was. She could educate him in all the ways the world disappoints. She could literally raise him and prepare him like she wished somebody would have prepared her.

She mulled over the paperwork that was sent with the young baby. She read about his appearance and for the first time she started examining the child for herself. She was actually very happy with his odd features because she felt like it would be easier to teach him isolation. For him, it would probably come naturally because he had been dealt a pretty crappy card in the looks department. As she read the bio on his birth mother she was actually offended. "What a real piece of work she was," Ethel sneered. Ethel was judging Ms. Damion almost as if she had no idea how far gone she herself really was. Christofer's bio wasn't very long, but after finishing it, Ethel had a sense of optimism. Teaching this child how the world really was would be very easy. So far, he seemed to have struck out in every situation he had been placed in. It must be a world record, since he was only three days old.

"Christofer Damion, what a stupid name," Ethel mocked, "it's not even spelled correctly."

She closed the file and stared at the now sleeping child. He had finished his bottle and had fallen asleep. She removed the bottle and used the blanket to cover him back up. Carrying him, quite carefully this time, she said his name over and over in her head. No child that she was going to raise would ever have such a stupid name.

Long ago, when dreams and hopes were still a part of her

and Ryder's lives, children were always a discussion. They wanted a whole litter of them. Ryder only had one request. He would name their first son. She hadn't thought about children with Ryder in a very long time. It was just too painful. Now upstairs, she placed the infant in a shallow laundry basket that was next to her bed.

"Better than the floor," she mumbled.

She covered him again with that same dingy blanket he was delivered with. The last hour had taken so much out of her, she decided she too needed to go to sleep. She crawled into bed and pulled up her thinned-out comforter all the way to her chin. She lay on her side, staring at the sleeping child. He looked so peaceful, she longed for sleep like that. She thought of nicknames she could call him. She couldn't believe that after all these years, she had a newborn in her home. Their home. Their dream. With Ryder on her mind, she closed her eyes. His one request, she could actually make happen. She smirked a little at the thought of doing something to honor her love.

"Goodnight Sebastian," she whispered.

Chapter 3: Life's Little Lessons

Ethel had the most exhausting night. She had never had a newborn before and didn't realize they required so much attention. For something so small, it sure did like to wake up and eat. For something so small, it sure did require a lot of diapers too. What the police department sent over would definitely not be enough. She would have to send for more supplies before the day was up. She refrained from holding the baby as he ate. She was nervous about breaking him, but she was also nervous about the way it would make her feel. She couldn't say the baby was cute, but there was something about him she was drawn to. She needed to develop a routine now. With Sebastian around, her normal hobbies of wallowing in despair probably wouldn't cut it. She didn't want to interact with him a lot, but she knew he would require a lot of care. She was already counting down the days until he would be able to look after himself. She strapped him in his car-seat and that became like his own personal animal cage. She did make sure he was clean and fed, but other than that, there was not much love shown to Sebastian.

"Sebastian," she smiled as she said his name out loud. "I want to teach you how the world actually is," she said matter-of-factly. "Nothing belongs to you, and it never will," she sneered.

Sebastian's empty stare back at her told her he had no idea what she was talking about, but she knew she would need to start at a very young age. Sitting in her living room, with the baby next to her in his car-seat, she wondered how long she would be able to do this. Two years was her limit, but with what she wanted to accomplish, she actually pondered if two years would be long enough. Sebastian let out a long scream that broke her concentration.

"Oh, for heaven's sake, what could it be now," she moaned.

He didn't need a diaper, he just had a two-hour nap, he must be hungry, she deduced. Making the last 6 oz left in his bag, she needed to get more. Twenty-years is a long time for bad habits to set in. They certainly had for Ethel. However, without her even realizing, this child was already changing her. She phoned the service and told them there were several baby items she needed. As she began to recite the list, she realized she didn't know what he needed. She had never raised a child; she didn't know what to get. She had a very delicate task in raising him exactly the way she wanted, so she knew she would need to take matters into her own hands. She canceled the service and hung the phone up abruptly. It had been twenty years, but Ethel was going out. Terror set in, as she threw on her overcoat. She didn't bother to change her slippers, but she sure didn't want to freeze. She was actually going out into the cold and bitter world. The world that didn't believe in true love. She put the car-seat on the floor.

"Toodles, Gypsy, and Rioooooo," she sang out. "Be momma's sweet dears and keep an eye out for Sebastian while I am away," she ordered.

All three cats looked up at her, almost as if they understood. Toodles, the smallest of the three, turned and crawled on top of baby Sebastian's lap. He turned two times and lay down.

"That's momma's good boy," Ethel purred. "I'll be back soon, and I'll even bring you back something special."

With that, she walked out of the living room and down the stairs.

She returned to the house a couple hours later. With clothing, diapers, and formula in tow, she felt like she had accomplished a lot. She received so many ugly stares while walking down the street, it was a painful reminder of how cruel the world was. She was grateful that due to her drastic change in appearance nobody had recognized her. This eliminated the list of questions she was certain would be asked if they had recognized her.

How are you, we are so sorry for your loss, and her favorite, we know what you are going through.

Nobody knew. Nobody could understand what this felt like. She walked over to Sebastian who was fast asleep. Tickling Toodles chin, she kissed his nose and told him how much of a good boy he was for taking care of the baby. She left all the items she just purchased on the table and sat down on the couch. Joining Toodles, Gypsy, and Rio, fifteen other cats started coming into the living room. She coaxed all of them to the couch and made sure to pat each one of them. These cats, they were the only things that never left her. They came in from the harsh world and needed shelter. She offered that, and they genuinely seemed grateful. None of them left, ever. When one would pass away, she would just add them to the cemetery outside the orphanage she had started many years ago. After Ryder, she knew these felines were the only ones who truly understood her. She might not have had kids of her own, but she knew she was their momma. They knew it too.

She put her feet on the coffee table and slunk back into the couch. The day had burned all her energy and she was ready to rest. She closed her eyes. Within seconds, Sebastian was awake, crying, and ready for a diaper change. Annoyed and reluctant, she got up and did what had to be done. This was going to be harder than she ever imagined.

Nine months old became her favorite age. Sebastian was finally sleeping through the night. He was more self-sufficient and had even learned how to use his right arm to hold the bottle, and his much shorter left arm as a support for his right arm. He was crawling, more mobile, and even had the goofiest grin. He babbled to Ethel all day; she never returned the conversation. He also babbled at the cats, and always to his delight, they would meow and purr back. Despite how hard she tried to show him how cold the world could be, he was relentless. He was always at her feet, tugging on her nightgown, and even trying to give her kisses. At times, she found herself caught up watching him play with the cats, she didn't even realize when she was smiling and laughing. How funny he looked, and yet he didn't realize it. His appearance didn't bother him yet, and it didn't bother the cats either. They adored Sebastian. They slept with him, played with him, and even let him pull on their tails occasionally. This child had infiltrated her lair, and her faithful cats treated him as their new leader. She seemed almost tickled by this. She still didn't like to hold him, but she would pick him up and move him if he was in harm's way. Sebastian would get into everything, and she would always remind him that those things didn't belong to him. She would scold him and tell him nothing actually belonged to him. She didn't allow him to have things. She needed his life to be empty. Although he no longer just sat in his car-seat, nine months was still her favorite age.

How quickly his first birthday came. He had a winter birthday, which at first, she didn't like. However, it made the task of isolating the child easier when she associated his winter birthday with the icy death of Ryder. It helped motivate her to continue treating him how she was. They didn't do much in celebrating his birthday, but a new stray wandered into the orphanage that day. Ethel was sure to remind Sebastian; the cat didn't belong to him. The night of his birthday, he took his first steps. Ethel was holding Rio on the couch, and Sebastian stood up by the coffee table and took two steps toward them. He immediately fell, and Ethel pounced to his side. She felt an odd sense of pride and protection course through her body. As she stood him back up, he looked at her with tear filled eyes and cried out, "Momma."

That one small word took Ethel's breath away and completely took her by surprise. Why did he just call her that?

She had never given him the idea that she was his mother. She barely talked to him; it was part of the developing process. Then it hit her like a ton of bricks. She always referred to herself as momma to her cats. Was it possible for such a young child to be so intuitive? Did he actually have the ability to associate those two things? Lord, did he think he himself was one of the cats? She never thought this far into her plan. She had a general idea of how things were going to pan out. The little moments of a child developing and growing never crossed her mind.

"Momma," the small child almost shouted, "momma." He reached his hands towards her this time.

She turned her back to him, "No," she quivered, "No momma!"

Sebastian grabbed her pinky with his little hand and said it again. She pulled away, this time with tears in her own eyes. She quickly grabbed a cat and put it in front of Sebastian to distract him. Although impromptu, the distraction worked, and Sebastian quickly became preoccupied.

At the age of two, the plan was really starting to come together. Ethel never got Sebastian anything to play with. He only had what she had, the cats. He would crawl around the third floor of New Hope finding all kinds of things to get into. One time, he managed to find an old button beside the fridge and he tried to eat it. Luckily, Toodles was there and was able to knock it out of his hand and paw it under the fridge. Ethel couldn't keep Sebastian out of things. He was definitely mobile now. His speech was incredibly advanced. This was so shocking to Ethel, she never had conversations with him personally. She spoke loads to her cats, and she just chalked Sebastian's speech to keen observation. He was fascinating that way. His inquisitiveness caused her to deep clean her loft. She hadn't cleaned like that, probably in twenty years. She did have to admit; the place was disgusting. It was nice to breathe in air that didn't smell like cat urine. She still didn't bother to address floors one and two of the orphanage, but she was impressed enough that the top floor was spic and span. When most children are beginning to learn shapes and colors, Ethel was teaching Sebastian fear and rejection. She had terrible games they played. In one of the games, she would put Sebastian in a closet and leave him in there for 20 minutes at a time. To make it more interesting, sometimes she would open the door like she was going to get him out, and then close the door and leave him in there for another five minutes. According to her, this bonus round would teach him rejection the best.

Sebastian hated this game. He spent the first ten minutes of it crying. Eventually, he would just lay on the floor and rock himself until Ethel unlocked the closet. Gypsy, the oldest of Ethel's cats, didn't seem to like this game much either. Every time they played, Gypsy always showed up. As soon as Ethel left the room, that fat gray tabby would come and lay in front of the door. It was as if he was trying to keep the child calm. Ethel knew this seemed harsh, but this was going to make him strong when it was all said and done. This particular game happened at least three times a week. As each week came, Sebastian would get more vocal about going into the closet. "No, don't wanna go," he would beg. He would kick and hit to keep from going in.

Ethel always won the fight. At the end of the twenty minutes, as long as she wasn't adding the bonus minutes, she would pull Sebastian out of the closet and talk to him. She told him how the closet was just like the world. In the world, bad things happen, and you are left all alone, in the dark to deal with them.

In her mind, she was completely justified in her actions. As long as she could teach him these lessons, she knew one day he would thank her.

On the night of the final day of year two, Sebastian lay in his bed sound asleep. This image made Ethel think back to the first night Sebastian was in her home. He didn't look as peaceful now as he had then. She knew she was doing a good job. She watched him take slow breaths as he slept. His orange hair was unkempt, and he still had a bit of dirt on his face. His right leg was outside of his space sheet, and she could see the holes in his sock. Gypsy, that old guard dog, was sleeping at the foot of his bed. Toodles, a bit more spastic, was curled up by his tuffs of hair, sharing his pillow. Even though this was never how she imagined her child rearing would be, she seemed content. She had a decision to make. If tradition held, she would phone the authorities in the morning to come and get Sebastian. She knew it needed to be done. Anything past two years was a recipe for disaster. She thought about all the little life lessons she had tried to instill over the last two years. He was still so young; she wasn't sure if he had quite grasped the pain yet. She thought about his first steps, his first word, and all the little things they had experienced together. Even with all the isolation, harsh words, and lack of items, Sebastian seemed to be somewhat happy just being there with her. She couldn't understand that sentiment and shuddered at the idea of her plan not working. She had to do right by this child, she had to teach him the truth. He had to have enough abandonment exposure to be able to face and handle the world. No, two years wasn't enough. He needed more time. She needed more time. She would have to break her own rule.

Sebastian was now three. It was a normal Tuesday at New Hope. The breakfast dishes were in the sink and Ethel was getting ready for one of her life lessons. It was time for the faithful, left in a closet game. Ethel went into Sebastian's room to get him. She couldn't find him at first. She looked in her room, the kitchenette, and living room with no luck. She hollered out for him but had no response. She checked the single bathroom in the upstairs loft, and still couldn't find him. A mild panic began to sink in and she started screaming his name. The last place she checked, she didn't really think he would be there. She checked anyway. Almost frantic, she swung open the closet door. Would he really volunteer to come here on his own? No, he wasn't there. She should have known, because Gypsy wasn't asleep in front of the door. Where could he be? She ran back into the living room and looked at the door that led to the stairwell. It was cracked. Surely, he didn't try to go down the stairs. He knew the rule. Never, ever leave. Her heart sank, he had never been on stairs before. Could a three-year-old even walk down stairs? She started wondering if she should have taught him this. She opened the door and yelled down the stairs for him.

"Sebastian, answer me right this instant," she cried out. There was no answer. She ran down the first set of stairs to the second floor. She hated being here. She hated the empty reminder of all the dreams she had lost.

"Sebastian, are you here?" she cried out.

No response. She quickly checked the entire floor and moved on to the last set of stairs. As she ran down the stairs, she felt a lump in her throat. She made it to the first floor and was out of breath.

"Hello?" she managed to squeak out.

She heard something this time. It was faint, but she heard it. It sounded like it was coming from the bathroom. She sprinted in that direction. There wasn't a light on, but the sun was shining through the broken windows. As she got closer, she heard him. He was whimpering and her heart skipped a beat. When she opened the door, the sight caught her off guard. There was little Sebastian laying on the floor and there was a puddle of blood coming from underneath him.

"Momma," he cried.

Fear overtook Ethel. What had happened to him, why was there so much blood? She never planned on doing what she did next, it just came naturally.

"Momma's here, baby," she comforted, and grabbed Sebastian and pulled him close to her, "Momma's here."

She hugged him so tight and then pulled him away to find the source of the blood. It wasn't as much as it had originally seemed. There was a small gash on the side of his head that was the culprit.

"What were you doing down here?" she questioned. "You know this was off limits," she continued. "What were you thinking? You scared me."

He looked up at her with his sad eyes and told her he just really wanted something to play with.

"You don't want me to have your things, momma. I was gonna find my own things." he whimpered.

When he had gone into the bathroom, he had slipped on some stagnant water that had leaked out from the rusted pipe underneath the bathroom sink. After slipping, he hit his head on the corner of the vanity, causing the gash. He was too scared to move, so he just lay there. Ethel listened to his simple explanation. She was the cause of this. This could have been so much worse. There could have been more than one way that he could have killed himself coming down those stairs. She was thankful for the small gash. All the times she caused him pain she felt it was necessary. She was only doing it for his own good. But this, this was something entirely different. He could have been seriously hurt, and it would have been her fault. She didn't expect to care as much as she did. Not knowing how to wrap her head around it, she got her and Sebastian off the floor.

"Let's go back upstairs and get you cleaned up," she coaxed.

For the first time, she carried Sebastian. The entire way he lay his head on her shoulder. She could feel his heart beating against her chest as they walked. That evening Sebastian didn't want to go to bed. Ethel was too emotionally drained to fight the persistent three-year-old, so she invited him over to her. He climbed in her lap again. He was just like a cat. Feed them once, they are your problem for life. She had held this kid only once in three years, and he just assumed that was an open invitation. Her first response was to push him off and say something ugly, but she held her tongue. His breathing slowed, and she could tell he was falling asleep. She welcomed this because she was ready for sleep herself. She thought back over the events of the day and was still disturbed about his injury. Why did she care so much?

As she carried him to his little bed, he held her tighter around her neck. He smelled like baby soap and Gypsy's flea collar. She lay him down and pulled the covers up closer to his chin. Gypsy had an uncanny way of knowing when it was bedtime and jumped passed Ethel to join his compadre for bed. The weight of Gypsy startled Sebastian and woke him a bit.

"Momma," he softly said.

She turned around and told him it was time to go to sleep. As she turned to exit, what Sebastian did next, Ethel never prepared herself for.

"I love you, momma," he said.

This stopped her dead in her tracks. He loves me? After everything that has happened, he loves me? She didn't respond and headed back to her bedroom. As she sat on the bed confused as to how this happened, she started crying. Her entire life came to the surface and she couldn't contain her emotions. In the room adjacent to hers was another little person who despite her best efforts, loved her. He loved Ethel despite her appearance and treatment of him. This pint-sized human showed Ethel unconditional love. She had only ever experienced that one other time in her life. This was never supposed to happen. In her calculation, it was never even a possibility. She closed her eyes thinking about those four little words.

Age three to four went by in a blur. Ethel stopped acting in tough love, and just loved. She read Sebastian stories, taught him his colors and shapes, and even let him name the new stray that came to the orphanage. Although Macaroni wasn't her first choice, she actually thought the name suited the orange tabby. She thought nine months was her favorite age, but she was wrong. She was having the time of her life. Sebastian was full of energy and wonder. She still didn't give him things, but they had each other so he didn't seem to mind. They even went outside. They did this often. They would take picnics, find animal shaped clouds, and even try to count the stars. The two were inseparable. Ethel loved watching Sebastian grow. It seemed as if every day he was changing. He looked less and less like a baby, and more like a big boy. His appearance was still odd, but she even found herself thinking he looked cute when he did certain things. His first painting hung proudly on the fridge.

One evening as they were finishing up dinner Sebastian was in rare form. He had so much energy he couldn't sit still. Ethel was losing her patience and she knew she needed to get him in bed immediately. Macaroni walked by and Sebastian threw a French fry at him.

"Get it boy," he said.

It was all Ethel could take.

"Go to bed," she ordered. "You have been bad all day. I can't handle anymore from you."

He slowly got up from the table, sulking as he went to his room. Ethel hadn't snapped like that in a while. It was the first time she had been negative since the injury. This once came easy to her, yet she was now worried that she had gone too far. She listened to see if she could hear his reaction, but his room was silent. She was nervous and went to see the outcome. When she got to his room, Sebastian had done as ordered and was lying in bed. She went and sat down beside him. Once again, his hair was unkempt and he had a little dirt on his face. She ran her fingers through his hair and started running through her head how she would try and explain herself to such a small person.

"I love you lots, momma, forever." Sebastian sighed.

She couldn't believe it. She was expecting him to be angry, sad, or upset. Instead, he once again proved his love for her. How could such a young person teach her such a big lesson? For the first time in twenty years, she couldn't believe she was going to utter these words.

"I love you too, Sebastian." Ethel replied.

Her plans had changed. She would still teach Sebastian that the world could be cold. She would still teach him that he had to protect himself because bad things could happen. However, she was going to do it the right way. She wanted to show Sebastian the love and wonders of the world Ryder had once showed her. She tiptoed to bed, genuinely in awe of what had just transpired.

Ethel awoke to the telephone ringing. It was 7:30 in the morning, who could this be? The phone never rang that early. She was still half asleep when she answered. "Great news, Ms. Ethel," the voice almost sang on the other line.

It was way too early for such excited conversation, she thought.

"We have done it, we found him a home."

What was this man talking about? Who were they talking about? Before she could ask those questions, the voice on the other end continued his excited conversation.

"We will be there around 11:00 today to get him. Don't you worry about a thing. We appreciate your dedicated service in taking care of him thus far. Christofer will be with his forever family before dinner! Isn't that excellent?"

She still wasn't making sense of what was being said. Christofer, that name did sound familiar. All of a sudden it hit her, and she shot up in bed. Christofer Damion was Sebastian. This man was talking about Sebastian. Her Sebastian.

"What are you talking about?" she questioned. "Who is coming to get Seb, er, I mean Christofer?"

"Don't you worry about a thing, we got it all worked out, the papers were signed yesterday evening. No need to pack anything for him, this family has got it all. Ok, you take care now, we will see you very soon."

The line disconnected. This had never happened to her before. She called to have children removed, it was never the other way around. She couldn't lose Sebastian. Not after everything they went through. She was his momma; she was going to be his forever home. She got on the phone with her lawyers, but it turns out even her amount of money couldn't touch what this new family had. They wouldn't tell her who they were, where they lived, or even if there were any other children in the home. She was just told that she had never signed any documents taking Christofer Damion in other than temporary placement. She was told it was a miracle that this family was even interested, and she should be happy that he was going to such an incredible home. As she looked around the loft, she knew it wasn't much, but he loved her. Irony is so cruel. All the years she spent pushing him away and teaching him rejection and isolation, it might actually come in handy today. She couldn't do it; she couldn't tell him he was leaving. Instead she woke him up with a song. They made his favorite breakfast and she even surprised him with his very own toy.

"A toy for me, oh thank you, momma." He squealed with delight.

It was just an old wooden car, but Sebastian acted as if she had just given him the moon. She made the most of those three hours, cherishing every minute of it.

It was like a replay of four years previous. She heard the car pull into the driveway. She wondered if good ole Officer McDonald was here to collect her son. She grabbed Sebastian's hand and walked down the stairs with him.

"Where are we going, momma?" he questioned.

"It's a surprise," she sniveled.

As they approached the vehicle, she didn't want to let go.

"Hiya Chris, I'm Officer Dash, it's nice to meet you," the officer said as he stuck his hand out.

Before Sebastian could even respond, Ethel interrupted.

"His name is Sebastian," she prompted.

"Paperwork says here that this is one Christofer Damion," remarked the officer.

"His name is Sebastian," she sternly urged.

The officer looked at the very confused child and caught on.

"Oh right, Sebastian, I see that right here," he corrected.

Ethel got on her knee and turned Sebastian towards her.

"Look sweetie, I love you ok, but this nice man is going to take you to a new family, who can give you more than I can. I need you to be a brave boy and go with him. Ok, can you do that?" Ethel managed to get it all out without shedding a tear.

"What, momma? What you talkin bout," Sebastian whined. "I want you, momma."

She couldn't bear to hear the tone in his voice. She thought she had prepared him for a moment just like this, but she could see in his eyes he felt the pain, but he didn't understand. He was still too young. This was too much for him. She couldn't handle this either.

"You have to go, baby, you have to go and be a good boy." She cried now.

Sebastian started crying loudly. He didn't know what she was talking about. She was all he knew. This home, these cats, and his momma. Why did he have to leave? Why did she want him to go? The officer stepped in and put his hand on Sebastian's shoulders.

"It's time to go, son," he motioned towards the car.

Sebastian broke free from his grasp and ran to Ethel nearly knocking her down.

"Momma, no." he cried uncontrollably.

She sobbed and just said she was sorry over and over. Officer Dash stepped forward, put his arms around Sebastian and picked him up. Sebastian didn't go without a fight and was wildly kicking his legs to try and break free.

"I want my momma, I want my momma," he hollered.

As he put Sebastian in the car, Ethel heard words that sent chills down her spine.

"You don't belong to her and she doesn't belong to you." the officer snapped.

All those years of saying those words herself, hearing them out loud was more than she could bear.

She watched as the squad car pulled down the beat-up drive, under the near-death Hawthorns. What had happened to this place? How had things gotten so out of hand? What was the point of anything anymore? As she walked around to the back of the property, her heart felt as if it was gone again. She had lost two loves. She never thought she would recover from Ryder and she almost hadn't. She never expected to feel love for Sebastian, but she did. The tears hadn't stopped since she told Sebastian he had to leave. It was like her shut off valve was broken. Gypsy, Toodles, and Rio had come outside but that still hadn't changed her disposition. She finally made it to the spot she was looking for. She hadn't been here in a very long time. At the very corner of her property was a place of rest. There were about five of her beloved cats who had passed away buried here. The most important part though, was the grave of her Ryder. A bouquet of dead butter weeds still lay on the headstone from past years of visits. She realized she hadn't been since the day Sebastian was delivered to her door. The pain of Ryder and Sebastian hit her like a flood. She lay on Ryder's grave crying uncontrollably. The pain in her chest tightened. How could she go on now? Why did she keep Sebastian past the two years? This never would have happened if she would have sent him away. She knew it was a mistake. It is not better to have loved and lost. She had loved desperately twice and lost twice. As she continued crying, Macaroni came from the orphanage and joined her at the gravesite. This was Sebastian's cat. He had named him. Just the sight of him was too much. Her heart literally had nothing left in it. Lying on Ryder's grave, at the corner of a property that overlooked a field of butterweeds and Hawthorns, Ethel died of a broken heart and joined her first true love.

Chapter 4: Too Good to be True

Officer Dash and Sebastian continued down the road. Officer Dash turned up the radio and hummed along. It was as if he was completely unaware of the shattered heart sitting behind him. Sebastian played it over and over in his head. Why did his momma make him leave? What had he done that was so wrong? He tried to be good, he tried to do everything she wanted. Why did she give him this toy just to get rid of him? He didn't want that stupid car. He just wanted his momma. He threw the toy in the floorboard and let out a huge sigh. He still couldn't wrap his small mind around everything that just happened. He just wanted to go back to his momma and his house. Why did the Officer tell him she didn't belong to him? Why did his momma always say that too? He had no idea why this was happening to him. It started raining. It was almost as if the sky felt the same despair that was swirling inside his tiny body. He lay his head on the window of the squad car and stared outside watching the trees as they zoomed by. The sight of them hurt his head. Between the tears, the stress of what just happened, and the sight of those trees, his head was killing him. He didn't want to think about any of it anymore, so he closed eyes and drifted into sleep.

Sebastian had been asleep for at least six hours. The feeling of the car driving on the road had soothed him enough to put him in a deep sleep. He only woke, because the car had come to a hurried stop. It jolted him a bit and startled him awake. They were parked in front of the biggest house he had ever seen. He thought it was incredible.

"Well, here we are kid. This place is a sight to take in, ain't it?" questioned Officer Dash.

It really was miraculous. This mansion appeared more like a castle. It stood about 180 feet tall. It was light gray in color but was adorned in royal blue accents. It was a wide home but had many levels to it. The tallest level had a window that overlooked the front, with a private balcony. It seemed to stand out above all the other levels. There were so many windows in the home. Each window had a unique design in it. The center window above the door had the prettiest stained-glass. There were family flags flying above six of the levels. No doubt, a very wealthy and special family lived here. Sebastian just stared in awe; he had never seen anything like this before. Officer Dash opened the door and coaxed Sebastian out.

"It is time to meet your forever family," he smiled.

Sebastian was offended by this. He didn't understand why he had to have a new family to begin with. As they approached the door, it was another work of art. It was deep mahogany with iron latches. Above that, a clock was built right into the concrete wall of the mansion. Above the clock was another balcony. Staring in amazement, the door slowly began to open. The light that poured from the inside almost seemed brighter than the sun itself. It blinded Sebastian. When his eyes finally focused, there were two people standing in front of him. They were holding hands and smiling.

This must be a momma and a dadda, Sebastian thought to himself. He only had a momma, but she had told him that some kids have both. He was curious about how that worked. He realized he was staring at the woman. His momma was special, but this lady was so beautiful. Her golden hair was pulled up neatly into a bun. She was wearing a blue dress and a white apron. He wasn't sure what she was doing in it, it was spotless. She had fair skin and the bluest eyes. They mimicked the outside color of the home. She had a sweet smile and a very cheery disposition.

"Well, hello there, handsome guy, we are so pleased to welcome you," she greeted Sebastian.

Sebastian didn't know how to respond; people weren't usually so pleasant when they first met him. He had remembered in the last year his momma told him to be a gentleman and shake hands. He had never done that before. He didn't really know the proper way to do it. Without thinking, he extended his short arm to shake the lady's hand. He had forgotten about his deformation and was immediately uncomfortable. He pulled his hand back quickly.

"That's ok, bud, it is part of what makes you special," the man next to her interrupted.

Sebastian had only ever met a man two times in his life. One was when he was young and all he could really remember about him was his smell and smile. Then, there was the officer he just spent the last two in-a- half-hours with, and he was not a fan. Sebastian didn't know how to take this new man. However, something about him made Sebastian feel safe. He was very tall and had pitch black hair. He had two dimples in his cheeks and he too had a great smile. His eyes were green and felt so kind. Sebastian slowly lifted his crippled arm back up, and the man shook his hand fervently.

"That-a-boy," he beckoned. "Don't be shy, you're home."

Well, Sebastian didn't feel like he was home, but he was hungry, and these folks seemed nice enough to at least feed him. He was still trying to think of a way to convince these people to take him back to his momma. Eating some food first wouldn't be a crime though.

"Could I please have some food?" Sebastian stammered.

"Oh heavens, of course," beamed the lady. She turned to her husband and instructed him to see the Officer out.

"Before I go," stated the officer, "I just needed to iron out some of the details. There seems there was some confusion with the paperwork. This here boy is named Sebastian, not Christofer. His foster mother was very persistent that we had made a mistake. I will be honest, after looking at what this kid has gone through, the last thing I was worried about was getting in a tiffy over a name."

Sebastian had no idea who this Christofer character was. Of course, his name was Sebastian, why would he think his name was something else? Sebastian also wanted to know how the officer seemed to know things about him. He had never met this man before this morning. He was glad they got his name figured out. He definitely didn't want these strange people calling him Christofer.

"That is fine by us, Officer Dash," the man interrupted Sebastian's thoughts. "Sebastian is a mighty fine name."

Sebastian watched as the man and the officer walked down the stoned pathway back to the squad car. The lady squatted down next to Sebastian and put her hand on his shoulder. He felt a warmth run through his body. She touched him so softly.

"How about we go find you some food now," she interjected. Sebastian just nodded his head yes, that sounded so good to him. She reached down and grabbed the hand of his good arm and started walking him inside. Panic set in for Sebastian. He thought he had made up his mind, but he was wrong. He pulled free from her grip and turned and ran back towards the car.

"Now wait a minute, kid. We already talked about this," groaned Officer Dash.

He stepped towards Sebastian and the man stood in between them.

"Give him a second, will ya?" he confronted the officer. Sebastian was shocked that this stranger stood up for him like that. Sebastian ran past the two men and opened the back door to the squad car. He jumped inside.

"Oh great, now I am gonna have to pull him out," whined Dash.

Within seconds, Sebastian emerged again from the car. Without even looking back at the two men, he slowly walked back towards the door. He was clinching that wooden toy car closely to his chest. He did want that stupid toy. He was planning on him and his momma playing with it as soon as he got back home.

He trotted back up to the lady who was still waiting for him.

"What do you have there, sweetie?" she sweetly asked.

He ignored her and continued through the now open door. She, joined with her husband, followed behind him. When he stepped through the door he couldn't believe his eyes. This place was even more incredible on the inside. He stepped into what appeared to be a foyer. Directly in front of him was a grand fireplace. It was built from the same material as the outside of the home, but the mantle was wrapped in a dark leather. There was a fire going and it warmed the entire front entryway. The same family crest that was flying outside was framed and mounted above the fireplace. A rich burgundy carpet lined the center of the alternating beige and cream tiles. The ceilings seemed to go on for miles, and there were several stone columns that framed the entrance into a very long hallway. Overhead were two chandeliers that each seemed to be the size of a small vehicle. The lights twinkled through the crystals and danced along the walls and onto the floor. Sebastian just turned in circles taking in the beauty of the place. This was not at all like his humble third floor back home.

"This way," the woman gestured.

They continued down the hallway on the same plush burgundy carpet from before. Alternating family photos and sconces lined the hallway. Everything seemed intricately placed. In almost every photo something caught Sebastian's eye. He hadn't seen or met a little girl in the house yet, but there she was on the wall. She had the same color eyes and hair as the lady who was leading him down the hallway. He wondered how come she wasn't with this couple. He wondered if that is why he was now here.

"Who's that?" Sebastian stuttered.

"Oh, in due time," reassured the man.

At the end of the hallway were two double doors. They stood about twelve feet tall and matched the same blue color as the exterior. Each door housed a metal cursive *D*. Sebastian didn't understand the significance to this. The doors opened to a grand dining room. A glass table and oversized burgundy chairs centered the room. It was set for a family of ten. It seemed as if it had been set for a party, but after seeing everything else, Sebastian knew this is how this family probably always ate. In carrying on with the theme, the plates, silverware, and even the napkins folded like tiny doves were the same blue that echoed throughout the home. Blue forks, Sebastian couldn't believe it. Sebastian traced his fingers along one of the chairs. Each chair was carved in ornate designs.

"Have a seat, bud," urged the man. "We will go get you some food."

Sebastian was overwhelmed and decided not to argue. He didn't care what they were bringing, at this point he would eat three-day old leftovers. There were two glasses at each place setting. They were so clean, they were shiny. He peered into one of the glasses at his setting and his face seemed to grow two sizes bigger. He stuck his tongue out. The sight made him giggle. He was getting distracted and needed to stay focused. He slid down from his chair and climbed under the table. As he lay on his back, he looked up through the table. There were so many place settings. This was such a nice house. It didn't matter. He wanted to go back to his momma, she must be worried. She must miss him. The last year he had been with her she had taught him so much. He learned quickly too. There was still a lot his mind didn't understand, but he knew what he felt, and he knew he wanted to go back to her. He could hear the lady and man in the kitchen. They were laughing. He could hear pots and pans banging against each other. Every once in a while, you could hear the lady tell the man to stop it and be serious. Although it sounded like a serious thing to say, she seemed to be saying it with humor and love. He thought they seemed to really like each other. They had certainly been nice to him. Shaking the thought of them away from his head, he started thinking about how to go home. He didn't actually know how he would be able to do it. He realized he didn't even know where he was, or how far from his momma he was. He had decided he would just eat, maybe even take a bath, and then just ask them to take him back. He thought it might work. After all, they didn't really know him. Why would they just take him from his momma and not give him back? Why did they think he wanted to be there in the first place? He decided that is exactly what he would do.

He climbed back out from under the table. He could still hear them clanking around in the kitchen. He walked to the other side of the dining room to look at another huge fireplace. This one was identical to the first. He had never seen a fireplace before, and now at this house he had already seen two. The bright orange and yellow flames almost danced inside the hearth. The image of them captivated him. He leaned in closer to them and could feel his cheeks growing warmer. He didn't understand but something inside of him wanted to touch the flames. He knew they were probably hot because he could feel the heat intensifying, but he didn't care. He lifted his left arm slowly towards the flame. He inched his hand closer and closer. He just wanted to run his fingers through the flames. Due to how short his arm was, he had to get very close to the flames. As he got closer, a bead of sweat dripped down his neck.

"Sebastian, dear, what on earth are you doing?" The lady jolted him out of his trance. "Fire is hot, dear, it could really hurt you!"

She walked over to Sebastian, placed her hands on his shoulders and guided him back to the table. She helped him get back into the big chair and unfolded the tiny dove that was once set beside the large plate and placed it in his lap.

"I hope you like pasta," she stated. "I make the best pasta!"

The man had joined them back in the dining room and looked as if he too was going to be eating. She spooned some pasta on his plate and stepped back.

"Go ahead, dear, dig right in." she urged.

Sebastian realized she was probably going to stand there the whole time he was eating. He didn't care. He was starving. As he shoveled spoonfuls of the cheesiest pasta he had ever eaten into his mouth, he had to admit, it was very delicious. She seemed elated that he was enjoying it. She left to grab him some juice as he finished.

"Can I have more?" Sebastian stammered.

"Of course, Bud!" the man rang out.

Sebastian realized he might not have heard that his name was Sebastian. He sure was stuck on calling him bud. Oddly enough, Sebastian almost didn't mind it. While he was starting on his second plate of pasta, he found himself staring at the flames again. Trying not to focus on them, he shifted his eyes up the fireplace. Then he saw it. He wasn't sure how he missed it before. Framed on top of the mantle was the biggest picture he had ever seen. It was of that same little girl he saw in the hallway. She looked about twice his age. She had on a very pretty blue and white dress. Her blonde hair was pulled back with a black ribbon. She had on earrings and shoes that were also black. The thing Sebastian liked the most was her smile. She almost seemed like she was laughing in the photo. As he continued to stare at it, he could almost hear her laughter. This made him smile. In her hands she was holding a rabbit! It was so small, Sebastian almost didn't see it. He had seen rabbits in the wild before when he and his momma had been on picnics. He had never seen someone who owned one. She was holding it, like he used to hold Macaroni. *Was this rabbit her cat*, he wondered.

He wanted to see this girl. He wished she was here with this man and woman. He figured it wasn't likely, because if they had her, why would they have brought him here. He shrugged his shoulders and continued eating his pasta. He found himself taking second glances at the photo of that little girl.

"Beatrice," once again the man had interrupted his thoughts. These people were really good at that.

"Her name is Beatrice," he said as he pointed to the picture.

"Beatrice," Sebastian echoed.

He liked that name. He didn't dare question where she was. The lady walked over to the man and kissed the top of his head.

"Let's just get him settled tonight. Tomorrow, once he is comfortable, we will address that. I don't want to overwhelm him on day one."

The man kissed her hand and shook his head in agreement. Great, what were they talking about now? Sebastian thought about the woman saying something about him settling for the night. He didn't know what "settling" was, but he knew he wasn't planning on being there through the night. He finished his pasta, finished his juice, and then worked up the nerve to ask them to take him back.

As he began to stand up, he heard the faintest whisper.

"Get back here, you silly rabbit! We aren't supposed to come down here tonight."

He had no idea where it was coming from. He looked at the woman whose eyes were now very large.

"You are going to get me in so much trouble, come back here now."

He heard again in a hushed voice. He found the source. It was coming from the open doorway that led to the kitchen. Within seconds, a small white rabbit hopped into the dining room right at Sebastian's feet. Without hesitation, the blonde-headed girl dove on top of the rabbit. Giggling as she rolled over, she had the rabbit cupped in her hands.

"Gotcha!" she exclaimed.

Sebastian was taken back. It was the girl from the photo.

The one whose smile made Sebastian feel happy inside. Laying on her back, she quickly realized what had just transpired and where she was. She slowly rolled to her belly, dropped her head and addressed the lady and man.

"Gee, I'm sorry, Mom. Sorry, Dad., I had to get Mr. Bunny," she explained.

She then turned towards Sebastian. She lifted her head and was eye to eye with Sebastian who never made it off the chair.

"Hi there, I'm Beatrice," she grinned.

Chapter 5: Settling In

That grin! He couldn't believe the girl from the photo was standing right in front of him. He really couldn't believe that the rabbit from the photo was real too. She even had a name for him. Mr. Bunny! It wasn't as good as Macaroni, but he was still impressed by them both.

"Did you hear me? I'm Beatrice," she echoed.

He quickly realized he was staring at her and he felt his cheeks redden.

"I'm Sebastian," he whispered while sticking his right hand out this time. He wanted to perfect this handshaking business.

"Sebastian?" she questioned as she looked toward her parents. They both nodded simultaneously.

"Sebastian, it is!" She cheered enthusiastically.

He was still waiting for her to shake his hand, when she did something that nearly knocked him off his chair. She leaned forward and hugged him. This stranger, who had a smile that made him feel as happy as his momma did, hugged him. Without hesitating, he put his arms around her back and hugged her back. The rabbit wriggled between the two of them which made them separate and start giggling. This had been by far the strangest encounter he had ever had with anyone. This had also been his favorite. He had no idea how to explain this feeling that he had being near this girl. She was a little person like him, she loved animals like him, and she made him feel normal. He really liked the feeling. He remembered where they were and again felt his cheeks getting warm. He looked around the room and everyone seemed to be staring at him. This would have normally made him feel uncomfortable, but they were all smiling.

"Mom, you made mac and cheese, that's my favorite," squealed Beatrice. "Could I have some too and finish eating dinner with Sebastian, please?" she begged.

"Well the cat's out of the bag now," said the man. "I say the more the merrier."

"More like the rabbit's out of the hat," laughed Beatrice.

Her laughter filled the room. The mom left the dining room and came right back with more pasta. Sebastian had previously decided to stop eating and proceed with his plan on getting back home, but something inside him wanted to stay and eat with Beatrice. He figured a little longer wouldn't hurt.

"Dad, can I sit next to Sebastian?" question Beatrice.

"Sure, sport," he replied.

Sebastian thought about this. This man had already called him Bud several times, and he was now calling Beatrice, Sport. He now knew that they did still have the girl from the photo with them, even though Sebastian was there too. He called her a nickname too; it wasn't just him. It wasn't just because he couldn't remember his name, he did it for his daughter too. Sebastian was so confused.

"You gonna finish your food, Sebastian?" interrupted Beatrice.

Her mom had returned and had already served Beatrice a bowl of pasta.

"It's mom's best dish, but she makes a lot you will like," beamed Beatrice.

Sebastian picked up his spoon and finished his second bowl. The four of them sat around the table for the next thirty minutes eating, talking, and laughing. Sebastian didn't actually say much during that time, he just enjoyed listening to the family. This was a dynamic he wasn't accustomed to, but he rather enjoyed how they interacted with each other. After they had finished eating, the lady made mention that it had been a very long day, and everyone should get cleaned up and head to bed. They would answer all the questions that needed to be answered in the morning over breakfast. Almost as if she had been summoned, a short, silver-haired, and rosy-cheeked lady entered the dining room.

"I gather you are all finished and ready for clean-up, my dears," stated the lady.

"Oh Nana, you are always right on time," gushed Beatrice. "Sebastian, this is Nana. She helps do everything around our house, you're gonna love her," continued Beatrice.

Nana was wearing all black and wore her hair in a tight bun. She moved very quickly, even though she was one of the roundest people Sebastian had ever seen. She had all the dishes picked up and out of the room almost within seconds. She never returned, but Sebastian could hear her cleaning up in the kitchen. She was a strange woman and Sebastian was intrigued.

"Ok kids, off we go, let's hit the hay," Beatrice's dad beckoned.

He walked over and scooped Beatrice up with one hand. He moved her to his back while she giggled and grinned. He held Mr. Bunny in his other hand and they headed back down the main hallway. Beatrice's mom walked over to Sebastian and grabbed his hand.

"Well, I can't do all of that, but I can certainly show you to your room," she sweetly interjected.

Hand in hand, they walked back down the hallway. Sebastian could still hear Beatrice giggling, and he wanted to know what she was laughing about. He wanted to spend more time with her. Through the hallway, the lady guided Sebastian into a winding corridor that spilled out near a grand staircase. The stairs were made of ivory and were lined with black carpet instead of burgundy. The handrails were made of black marble and looked hand carved. On either side of the stairs were matching black marble pillars that mirrored the height of the stairs. They were massive. The top landing was the most breath-taking. In the center of the landing, a large cursive D that mimicked the dining doors was woven into the carpet. Above the landing was another chandelier. It was even more impressive than the two downstairs. There were at least 5,000 crystals on this one. It hung from a dome shaped recessed roof that was also made of stained-glass. It displayed at least twenty types of flowers. This chandelier ricocheted colored light from the stained glass around the entire upstairs of the house. It was magical. There were four hallways off this main landing and Sebastian couldn't even see the end to them. They continued walking down a hallway until they reached the second door on the right.

"This is it, I can't wait for you to see this," gleamed the lady.

When she opened the large wooden doors, Sebastian was in awe. He stepped into a room that looked like it was meant for a king. There was a large Brazilian Rosewood sleigh bed in the center of the room. It was covered with plush navy and gold bedding. There were seven decorative pillows on top of that. The floor consisted of a navy and cream tile. Behind the bed was a wall of curtains made of gold silk. At the foot of the bed was a shelf full of toy cars. There had to be at least fifty brightly colored cars. He looked down at the wooden car he was still holding and walked over and placed it on the top shelf. Across from the bed was another fireplace. He couldn't believe there was one in this room. Past the fireplace, there was a huge bath-room. The bathroom had a shower and a tub. Above the tub was more stained-glass. These people really loved that stuff. In the corner of the room was a navy-blue desk. The wall adjacent to it was lined with bookcases filled tightly with books. Sebas-tian didn't know how to read yet, but the books in the room called to him. They were actually his favorite part. In the corner opposite of the desk was a huge hutch filled with toys. Sebastian had never seen so many toys. Once again, the lady interrupted his thoughts.

"Well, do you like it?" she questioned.

"It looks good," Sebastian replied."

"Well these are just a few things we put in here for you, we can always get you more if you need it," she continued.

"Get me more things?" Sebastian wondered out loud.

"Yes silly, everything in here is yours!" she explained.

Sebastian could not understand what she was talking about. They were serious about him staying here, very serious. He had to admit, the place was incredible.

"Ok, sweetie, Nana will be in to help you get cleaned up and tucked in. We have a busy day in the morning, and you need your rest. Sleep well. I promise, things will get easier," she reassured.

She exited the room before Sebastian could hesitate. He still wasn't planning on being there for the night. Within seconds, Nana had come into the room and did get him cleaned up. It was very awkward, but the bath water felt so good. She dressed him in navy blue silk pajamas and put him into bed.

"Try and sleep dear," she stated as she exited the room, shutting the door behind her. Great, now what was he going to do? If he left the room, he had no idea where the big people's room would be, he wasn't sure if he could even find the front door. The thought of spending the night started to upset him. He pulled back the covers and slipped out of the enormous bed. He tiptoed across the room to the door. He was hoping that someone would be laughing or talking so he could find them. No matter what, he had regained his courage to ask to go back home. He was grateful for the meal, the bath, and the jammies, but he still wanted to go home. As he neared the door, it started opening. This startled him so much, without even thinking, he sprinted back to the bed and jumped in it. To his surprise, Beatrice stuck her head in the door.

"Hey there, Sebastian," she grinned. "I just wanted to say goodnight. We are going to have so much fun together. There will be so many adventures. I am so glad you are here; I'll see you in the morning."

With that last statement, she left as quickly as she came. She said so much so quickly, Sebastian tried to process it all. They were going to have adventures together. Him and her. He didn't know why, but he really liked the sound of that. Maybe this girl could understand him better than anyone else had because she was a kid just like him. Although he loved his momma, he knew that every big person that had been in his life so far had let him down. What if Beatrice was different, he wondered. He decided it was late, and he could just stay one night. He might as well get some sleep and then he could just start fresh in the morning. He snuggled back underneath the plush blanket and started to relax. He drifted off to sleep thinking about that silly grin of Beatrice's.

Although he was only four and a half, Sebastian had already endured more than most adults could handle without giving up. Even though he couldn't grasp it, Sebastian was a survivor. Something inside that young yet inquisitive brain told him to fight. He didn't know it, but he was exhausted. Fighting while living had taken a toll on his mind and body. This was the first night's sleep in four years that Sebastian rested. He was relaxed, comfortable, content, and dare say, somewhat happy. Beatrice had overwhelmed him in a good way. He was sleeping so sound, he never heard Nana enter.

"Rise and shine," she almost sang out.

She drew back the curtains and light poured into the room. He covered his eyes with both forearms, hoping to cut out some of the light.

"I just want to sleep," Sebastian whined in reply.

"Nonsense, the sun is up, the birds are chirping, and there is a lot of life to live," chimed Nana.

"Breakfast will be ready very soon, and your clothes are already on the bed. I trust you will be able to slip on shorts and t-shirt without my assistance. I will stay outside the door to see you to the dining room as soon as you are dressed."

With that, Nana exited as quietly as she had entered. Sebastian just lay there for a few seconds trying to remember exactly what had happened yesterday. It was such a whirlwind of emotions. He remembered he wanted to go back to his momma and this motivated him to get up. He looked on his bed and there was a shirt and pair of shorts as promised by Nana. He quickly slipped on the khaki shorts and the deep purple striped shirt. He went to the bathroom and just stared at himself in the very large mirror. He could see the surroundings of the magnificent room behind him in the mirror. He knew he didn't belong here. This was not home. However, he enjoyed seeing himself in this environment. This was a room of a little boy who was loved. He couldn't shake that feeling. He knew his momma did some things that he hadn't liked, but he knew she loved him. He felt the love, especially towards the last year he had with her. He started wondering if there were different kinds of love. His momma didn't have a husband, so she didn't have the kind of love the man and woman downstairs seem to share. His momma didn't have a daughter, so she didn't have the kind of love this lady had for Beatrice. So, he wondered if maybe his momma's love, though very scary and hard at times, was her kind of love. He pondered if maybe these people could show him a new kind of love. The loud growling of his stomach shook the thoughts from his head. He ate so much pasta last night, how in the world could his stomach be acting like this? It bellowed out again, prompting him to head towards the door. He tried opening it, but it was much too heavy.

"Hello, Nana, are you still out there?" yelled Sebastian.

Without hesitation, Nana stuck her face in and guided him out of the room. She walked in front of Sebastian and he had to nearly jog to keep up with her. He thought to himself that she must always move at a speed like this. He tried to pay attention to the way they were headed to the dining room, so he could get a feel of the house, but after the first turn he was completely lost. As the duo approached the dining room, Sebastian could hear hushed voices. He couldn't make out how many people were in the room, but there was really only one person he was anxious to see.

"The young Sebastian for breakfast," Nana introduced.

He thought it sounded so silly for her to do this. Apparently so did Beatrice, because before he even saw her, he heard her laugh. He was so happy she was there.

"Good morning, Bud."

Sebastian had already learned to welcome this.

"Hope you slept well in your bed," greeted Beatrice's dad.

"I did, Mr." replied Sebastian.

"Mr! Ha, did you hear that mom? Sebastian gave me my very own nickname! I like it. You can call her Mrs. for now too. Good job, Sebastian."

Sebastian was a little confused by this transaction. He wasn't trying to give him a name, but rather was trying to address him with manners like his momma had taught him but realized he didn't know their names.

"Very clever indeed," added Mrs.

Sebastian didn't dare argue, he needed these people on his good side.

"Hey, what about me Sebastian?" pouted Beatrice. "What do you want to call me?"

This startled Sebastian. He didn't know what to call her. He didn't really know how he fit into her life. He was just a guest in her house for a few more hours, if he had anything to do with it. He had actually never even said her name out loud. He didn't know what to say and just hung his head in shame. Mrs. came over and slipped her delicate hand under his chin. She slowly lifted his eyes and met his gaze.

"Dear, don't ever feel like you need to hang your head in this home. We want you here. You have as much right to be here as anyone else. Don't ever feel like any less than that. I want you to always hold your head with pride."

Sebastian was in awe at what he had just been told. Some of the things didn't make sense, but she seemed so genuine. He stared at her eyes the entire time she spoke to him. They were filled with the most kindness he had ever seen.

"Don't worry Sebastian, we've got plenty of time to think about it."

Let's eat, I'm starving," smiled Beatrice.

Right on cue, Nana entered with a cart that had four silver cloches on them. As she revealed each one, they were filled with meats, eggs, biscuits, and fruit. There were also three different types of juice, white milk, and chocolate milk. Sebastian's stomach let out a third growl. This one echoed in his ears, and he looked around quickly to see if anyone else had noticed. Nana plated up the food for the four of them. Sebastian wondered if Nana ever ate, because she never sat down with the family. As soon as everyone was finished, Nana disappeared again into the kitchen. Sebastian picked up his fork, still so amused by its color, and stuck it into a piece of sausage. As he lifted it to his mouth, he looked up and realized he was the only one eating. Quickly dropping his fork, he began to drop his head again. Mrs. cleared her throat before he could droop it all the way down. He made eye contact with her, as she grabbed Mr. and Beatrice's hands. She then reached for Sebastian's hand as Beatrice reached for the other. Beatrice grabbed his crippled hand without hesitation. The family closed their eyes and Sebastian followed suit. They prayed for the food, said 'Amen' in unison, and then began to eat. This was Sebastian's first experience with something like this and he didn't quite understand it. He figured there were probably several unique things this family did together. Breakfast lasted about an hour. Again, the family discussed things from groceries, news, and sports. Sebastian just soaked in the conversation. A few times they would direct their questions to him, and he would just shake his head no or yes in reply. Most of the time they were just asking him if he had ever done something or been somewhere. Usually his response was no. As Mr. finished his last piece of bacon, his phone rang. He showed the phone to Mrs. and then silenced the phone. As Nana emerged from the kitchen and started gathering the morning dishes, Mrs. stood promptly and whispered something to Nana. Nana nodded in obedience and set the plate back down.

"Come children, we are going to get washed up in the front bath, and then head to the garden," ordered Nana.

"I love the garden. Sebastian, you will too!" squealed Beatrice.

Nana took both children into the front bath and cleaned them up. She washed their faces, brushed their hair, and their teeth. She exited and told the children to sit tight, while she threw the dirty towels in the laundry.

Almost as if Beatrice was reading his mind, "You get used to it," she blurted out.

She was referring to Nana doing everything for them, and he was wondering how Beatrice was just standing there while Nana was fussing with them. Not to disappoint, Nana was back with lightning speed.

"Ok, to the garden and march," ordered Nana.

Beatrice skipped ahead down the long hallway. They were going into another part of the house Sebastian had never been. They turned and headed down another hallway. At the end of the hallway were about ten French doors. The wood had been painted gold. They almost sparkled in the sun. He assumed the garden was on the other side of the doors. This hallway was lined with the same plush burgundy carpet. Instead of family photos and sconces, this wall was lined with artwork. It was a peculiar collection. There were pieces of the High Renaissance that mimicked the great works of Da Vinci. These pieces seemed to be right at home. Their detailed work matched that of the home they were housed in. Each piece was more detailed than the previous. There were three pieces of Maritime artwork that all seemed to be depicting the same boat. Each background portrayed a different characteristic of the sea. They were less detailed, but still very breathtaking to look at. The last of the paintings were the most chaotic of the three and seemed the least likely to be in this house. It would best be described as abstract. It was vibrant, colorful, bold and completely messy. He thought this seemed to be an odd collection of artwork.

"These are the family's personal collections. They each painted these. You see the blank spots at the end of the hall? Those are for you. Once you complete your works of art, they will hang with the rest of the family's," explained Nana.

They had made a spot for him to paint and hang up in their house. It was those little things that kept pulling on Sebastian's heart. Now approaching the outside, Beatrice was already outside swinging on one of two swings hanging from a huge Oak tree. This was some garden. There were at least 100 varieties of floral life present. The family was also growing several types of vegetables and fruit. This was much different than the butterweeds back home. Their yard was perfectly manicured. Framing a courtyard, were hedges shaped like bunny rabbits. No doubt, this was at the request of the effervescent Beatrice. This backyard was the entire size of the property at New Hope. There was a wrought iron gazebo beyond the swings where Beatrice was. There was Harald Ivy growing all over it. It was also surrounded with different species of butterflies. To the right of the swings was a concrete bird bath. Inside the bath, a male and female cardinal almost seemed to dance. There were two squirrels on the oak who appeared to be fighting over an acorn. Sebastian could hear a woodpecker in the distance. Sebastian couldn't believe the backyard was as magical as the inside. No wonder Beatrice loved the garden. Although Sebastian was also enjoying being in the garden, his mind wandered back to what the Mrs. had said to Nana. It didn't seem as if it was the original plan.

"Come swing with me!" bellowed Beatrice.

Sebastian had actually never done that before and wanted to try it. He rushed over to the swing. Awkwardly climbing up, he made it onto the swing. It took him longer than he thought it would. Once he was up there, he realized he didn't know what to do.

"I can't do it," Sebastian sulked.

He wasn't sure how Beatrice would react and contemplated just getting off and running to hide in the gazebo.

"It's fine, I'll teach you," she reassured.

For the next few minutes, Beatrice patiently explained to Sebastian the trick to moving your feet out and in. She would prompt him when to do what. He caught on very quickly. Without much time passing, both children were swinging. Sebastian felt so free. He knew he wasn't, but he felt as if he was kicking the clouds, he was getting so high. The pair giggled and laughed while they swung together. They didn't even notice when Mr. and Mrs. had first come outside. Sebastian was watching Beatrice, when her sudden facial expression stopped him mid swing. She looked like she had just been punched in the gut. He didn't like seeing her like that.

"Children, go to the gazebo and have a seat, please," Nana instructed.

Beatrice dragged her feet on the ground to stop herself and grabbed Sebastian's rope to stop him. She slowly walked towards the gazebo, and not knowing what was going on, Sebastian just followed in tow.

Mr. and Mrs. were already sitting and waiting. As they approached, Sebastian could see they had bags with them. He wondered if they had decided to get rid of him after all. Although this is what he wanted, he couldn't think of what he had done wrong.

"You promised me this time would be longer," Beatrice sniffled.

She sat down next to Mrs. and put her head on her shoulder. The Mrs. wrapped her arm around her and rocked her.

"I know sweetie, but you know we don't really have control of it. When dad gets called, we have to go. It is how we have been able to provide this life for you. It comes with its own defaults," the Mrs. said trying to console Beatrice.

"Listen, Sport, this one may be for longer than what you are used to. It is the biggest project dad has ever done. It is also the most important. Nana will be here, and you won't be alone this time," Mr. reassured as he nodded towards Sebastian.

Sebastian still couldn't piece together what was going on. Why did he say Beatrice was used to being alone? She had two parents who adored her, how could she possibly ever feel alone? Noticing his puzzled face, the Mrs. invited Sebastian to sit next to her and Beatrice, so she could explain. She spent the next thirty minutes putting everything in perspective for Sebastian. Apparently, Mr. was a Neuroscientist on hire for the government. They wouldn't say what he did for the government, but just kept reassuring it was super important. Mrs. was also a Biotechnologist and was also doubly employed by the government. They were a package deal. They even told Sebastian they had their own private lab on the lowest floor of the house, but it was strictly forbidden. Nobody was ever allowed down there, they assured this was for everyone's safety. Travel was a necessary evil in their career. Based on Beatrice's reaction, it seemed as if it was also a frequent part of their career. They wished they were home more, but the sad truth was that Nana had done most of the raising of Beatrice. Unfortunately for Beatrice, since the house required so much attention, Mr. Bunny had become Beatrice's only companion. Although Mr. and Mrs. hadn't told the children how long they would be gone, Sebastian had an uneasy feeling it was going to be for quite some time. Mr. looked at his watch and beckoned his wife to get up and say goodbye. They both hugged and kissed Beatrice, who looked as if her world had just ended. When they approached him, Mr. ruffled his hair and promised they would make it up to him. Mrs. squatted down and placed her hand on his shoulder just as she had done 24 hours previously when he had arrived.

"We are so sorry this has happened. It was never part of the plan. We promise you will love it here. We are going to be a family; this is just part of the trials that come with that. Just know, we want to be here more for you, and we will always think of you and Beatrice while we are gone. We won't be able to call much, because where we are going, but we are thinking of you," she softly explained.

With that, she kissed the top of his head and hugged him just as she had done with Beatrice, who was still sitting in the same spot. As she joined Mr. at the entrance to the gazebo, they looked at the children one last time and turned to leave.

"Wait, I am going with you," Sebastian blurted out.

They both turned around in response.

"Oh, Bud, you can't, children can't go where we are going," instructed Mr.

"No, I mean, I want you to take me and drop me off at my house with my momma," Sebastian continued.

The look of confusion dawned both their faces. Sebastian was not prepared for the next reaction.

"You don't want to stay with me?" hollered Beatrice.

Sebastian whipped around to see a now crying Beatrice. She wiped snot from her nose and tears from her eyes. They continued dropping onto her pretty dress.

"We are supposed to stay together. I never see mom and dad anymore. You are supposed to be here for me," blubbered Beatrice.

Sebastian did not like her reaction. It hurt his heart. He hated that he was making her feel this way. He knew what this felt like all too well. She dropped down to the floor and just sobbed. He looked towards Mr. and Mrs. for guidance. Mrs. now had her head buried in Mr.'s chest, she too seemed to be weeping. "Bud, wouldn't you, maybe, like to stay here with us, with Beatrice?" coaxed Mr.

For the first time, Sebastian didn't seem as confident in his decision to leave. He was now torn. He wanted to go back to his momma, he missed her, but maybe she had a reason for letting him go. Maybe she knew something he didn't. He did have a desire to be near Beatrice. He had already had so much fun with her. It was too much for his young brain to try and sort out. He didn't know what to do.

"We were supposed to be brother and sister," whimpered Beatrice. "Why don't you want to be with me either?"

Sebastian took a step closer to the adults. Mrs. still hadn't looked up. Beatrice stood, dusted her dress off, and with tear-stained cheeks stepped towards them as well.

"Sebastian," she said softly, "I will always be here for you. We will always be together. Please stay. I belong to you and you belong to me."

Sebastian couldn't believe what he had just heard her say. He had always been told nothing belonged to him. He had always been told everything would be taken from him or everyone would leave him, and so far, that was true. Here she was. The exception to the rule. She wanted him to stay, so they wouldn't be alone ever again. She belonged to him and him to her. She said so herself. He thought of everything that happened to him since he could remember. His mind was swirling. He decided he had to go with his heart. He wanted new love. He wanted a sister; he liked the sound of that. He also couldn't bear to make her feel the way he had felt so many times in his young life.

"I wanna stay with you Bea," Sebastian quietly said.

Her glossy eyes met his, and her famous Beatrice smile started forming.

"That is the perfect nickname. I love it." she exclaimed.

Chapter 6: Hearts Knitted

Deciding to stay was a very hard decision for Sebastian. As he sat in his room, he still couldn't believe it all belonged to him. He fidgeted with the wheels on his toy car. It reminded him of his momma, and it was literally the only thing he had that did. There were no pictures or anything personal from his old home, just this little toy car. He knew if he was going to make this his new home, he had to let go of his past. He walked to his bathroom to throw away the car. He neared the trash can, still spinning the wheels thinking about his last year with his momma. The good year. He sucked in a deep breath and held the car over the trash can. He spun the wheel one last time and dropped it in the trash. He turned to leave the bathroom, and something halted his step. He couldn't do it. He couldn't let her go completely. He turned back around, reached into the trash can, and took that little wooden car out. He ran to his bed and stuffed it underneath. He decided he would just keep it out of sight, but not completely gone. This was the best compromise he could think of. Nana had made the children lunch and he was eager to see what there was to eat. He ran to the open door and out into the hallway. Once in the hallway, he remembered he still couldn't quite get around.

"Bea, where are you?" he cried out. "Bea, I don't know where I am going, I need your help."

He could see a light coming from a room about four doors down and he figured he would just head that way. He couldn't really get any more lost than what he already was. He tiptoed down the hallway, unsure of what this room would hold. This house, his house, had so many rooms and so many surprises. He felt anxious to explore them all. As he reached the door, he peered in slowly around the corner.

"You're still my bestest friend, Mr. Bunny, but I have a brother now," Beatrice sweetly said to her rabbit.

She opened his cage to put him in it. Sebastian couldn't believe his eyes, even Mr. Bunny had a cage reminiscent of a castle. It was made of aspen that had been painted white and was trimmed in navy accents. The entire thing was elevated at least five feet off the ground. The main compartment had an aspen bed lined in alfalfa hay for Mr. Bunny. The side compartments housed more bedding and cute little windows. Off the main compartment was a ramp that went below the compartments that had a caged in open area for Mr. Bunny to hop around in freely. This is where Beatrice had put him into the cage and Mr. Bunny was currently running up the ramp to his bed. Above the main compartment was another ramp and another level. The highest level was pitched and housed Mr. Bunny's water bottle and food dish. He had fresh veggies and what appeared to be apple slices to munch on. This rabbit was living a very good life.

"Hey, Sebastian, how long you been standing there?" Bea rang out.

He felt a little embarrassed to not have said anything and stepped inside her room.

"I don't really know how to get to the dining room yet," Sebastian said sheepishly.

"You'll adjust, I promise. We can walk down together, and I can teach ya my trick for remembering how to get around," Beatrice encouraged.

"I like your room," Sebastian smiled.

He really did like it. They had definitely spared no expense on this room. Bea told Sebastian she would give him the grand tour and began showing him around. Mr. Bunny's cage was on the far wall of the room. In the opposite corner, Bea's king-sized bed was positioned diagonally. As large as it was, it still didn't fill the ginormous room. The comforter on her bed was stark white and had gathers in it that were beaded. The bottom of the comforter was ruffled and nearly touched the floor. The colors of her canopy and bed skirt matched the curtains in the window. They were all made from silk and adorned a cream and ash blue alternating vertical stripe. The ends were decorated with gold fringe that gave them the most delicate touch. Beside Mr. Bunny's cage was a bay window which had a custom-built window seat. The seat had plush cushions of various shapes and sizes atop of it. On her main wall was an adorable wing back love seat in the same ash blue as the linens. It too had beaded gathers on it. There was a large area rug in the center of the room. It was detailed with flowers that also matched the colors of the linens. Her wall was covered in creamed damask wallpaper. Although she didn't have a fireplace, she did have an impressive chandelier. It matched the one on the landing that Sebastian had seen days before. Sebastian was looking for the stained glass. He knew there had to be some in the room somewhere. Bea also had a desk. It was white and had gold leafing on every drawer. She didn't have a toy chest, but she did have almost an entire art studio in her room. She had every art supply imaginable. There was an easel with a painting that was in the process of being done. Sebastian spotted the chaotic colors and knew he had found the maker of the abstract work in the second hallway. Beatrice took him to her favorite part in the entire room, her closet. When she opened the doors, it looked like an ordinary closet until they stepped in. The entire ceiling of the closet was made of stained glass. Sebastian knew it would be in here somewhere! Although he was impressed with the amount of clothing she had and the stained glass, he couldn't figure out why this was her favorite part of her room, especially compared to what he had just seen in the main room.

"Ok, are you ready?" Bea asked.

Sebastian just nodded; he wasn't sure what he was agreeing to. She pushed a box of hats and scarves over and there was a secret door behind it. It was only three-foot-high and about four-feet-wide.

"Be prepared to be amazed," Bea proudly proclaimed.

She lifted the hook from the lock and pushed the door open. She got on her hands and knees and crawled through the door.

"Come on," she yelled from the other side.

Sebastian couldn't believe what he had just witnessed. Her closet had a secret door to another room. He couldn't even imagine what was on the other side. Shrugging his shoulders, he followed Bea over. He had a more difficult time trying to crawl because of his short arm, so he dropped to his belly and slithered into the other room like a snake. The sight of him slithering made Bea giggle. Sebastian thought about how he must look, and he giggled too. Once he had made it, he stood and dusted his knees. He immediately fell in love with the room. He was standing in a room about three times the size of his. On all four walls, from ceiling to floor, were bookshelves full of books of all colors, sizes, and content. It was a sea of books everywhere he turned. He had just assumed his room had the most books one room could hold, but he was wrong. He knew about books. He couldn't read them yet, but he knew there were new adventures in every book. In the center of the room was a plush rug and a sectional leather sofa. The room had six chandeliers in it that lit every square inch. Each wall of books had its own ladder. Without him realizing it, Bea had already climbed on one of the ladders and was pulling a book off the shelf. She climbed down and beckoned Sebastian to the sofa. She showed him her favorite book. It was about a daring knight who rescues a helpless princess. Together they rule a kingdom honestly and faithfully. They go on adventures together and help to rid the kingdom of all dangers. She read a few of her favorite pages to

Sebastian. He loved listening to her read. She explained how this was basically just a library for the two of them because Mr. and Mrs. books were all in their lab, which she reminded him to never go into. She also told Sebastian that since she had learned to read, she spent most of her days in the library because she was all alone. The books made her feel like she had somebody. Sebastian could sense that he loved this room as much as she did, and he was happy that they already seemed to have things in common.

"Children, where are you?" Nana called. "It is past time to eat and the food is getting cold. I won't heat it up. So, either come down while it's still warm, or help yourselves to cold chicken nuggets and corn."

Bea giggled and jumped off the sofa.

"Ok, brother, we better hurry up before Nana gets in a tiffy," Bea instructed.

Sebastian just stared at Beatrice for a moment. She called him brother. He felt in his heart, she truly meant what she had said in the garden. They belonged together and would be together forever as brother and sister. The idea melted his heart. He followed her back through the secret door and out of her room.

"Hurry up, slow poke," teased Beatrice.

"Wait, the trick," Sebastian reminded.

"Oh yea, that's right," Bea started. "Ok, it's a song I used to sing. It has been a while, but I still remember it. It will help you remember quicker if you sing it."

She cleared her throat and began.

"You wanna eat, don't even fret. From my room take thirty steps. Go down the stairs and into a hall. Skip for fun, try not to fall. It seems long, but don't take a right, straight ahead, the food is in sight."

She finished singing and struck a pose. She seemed very pleased with herself. Sebastian was thoroughly amused by this.

"I have a song for all the main areas. Like I said, you only have to sing it until you get used to the house, which shouldn't take you very long. Now you try, I'll sing it with you."

Standing right outside Bea's room, Sebastian and Beatrice sang the song together. They sang it once for practice, and then sang it again as they moved to the dining room following the directions of the song. Sebastian had never sung before, and although it seemed silly at first, he had to admit it was catchy and did help him make it to the dining room. Not a moment too soon either, because Nana was standing in front of the doors with her arms folded across her chest.

"Go on now, dears, go eat, and when you are through, off to class with you."

Sebastian didn't know what class was, but he would worry about that later. Right now, he had lukewarm chicken nuggets and corn calling his name.

This dining room had quickly grown to be a favorite room in the house for Sebastian. He had already, in his short stay, created fond memories. He liked that he had more than one good memory to choose from. This idea made him happy as he grabbed his fork to eat. He had grown used to the fact that he was a kid who got to eat with blue silverware. He didn't know what Nana was talking about. Cold or not, the chicken nuggets were yummy. As he shoveled a huge spoonful of corn in his mouth, he was on the fence of whether he liked it or not. While continuing his food, Bea did the strangest thing that caught him off guard. Thinking back on it, it was very funny. Well, it was funny to the children, Nana didn't seem very amused. Bea picked up her fork and shouted *en garde*. Picking up on Sebastian's puzzled face, Beatrice quickly explained that he needed to grab his fork because she was challenging him to a culinary duel. He hesitantly grabbed his fork and she struck it. The metals clinked together and rang out. She did it again. *Ching*, the sound rang out again. She struck it a third time and Sebastian caught on. Within seconds, they had moved from the dining room table to the floor. They chased each other around the table, stopping only to fork-fight each other in between continuous laughter. On one of Sebastian's final strikes to Bea's fork, she dropped her fork, let out a grunt, and fell to the ground.

"You got me, partner," she bellowed. "I'm down for the count, you win."

Sebastian realized she was only teasing and giggled.

"Woo hoo, I'm the champion," he spun in victory.

Nana had entered the room in time to observe Sebastian's victory spin and cleared her throat.

"Are you two planning on celebrating by finishing your corn?" she questioned.

"Sorry Nana," Bea said, still laying on the floor. "I challenged Sebastian to a culinary duel, and he won."

She rolled over to her side and slowly got up.

"My pride is wounded, but I'll live."

Both children got back in their chairs and continued their lunch.

"Well, *lettuce* celebrate with some of my favorite strawberry cake," Nana jested.

"Hey, Nana, you made a joke," laughed Bea. "Too funny."

Nana left, and within seconds was back with two plates of strawberry cake and two cups of milk. The children scarfed the cake down quickly and then guzzled the milk. Much to Sebastian's surprise, the milk was also strawberry flavored. Sebastian was so amazed by this. He had no idea milk could come in different flavors. The strawberry cake and strawberry milk were truly the best thing Sebastian had ever tasted. Which in this house was hard to beat, because so far Sebastian had enjoyed every meal he had eaten. The children were practically licking their plates clean when Nana reemerged to clean up. She reminded them that they needed to hurry, or they would be late for class.

Still not sure what she was talking about, Sebastian wiped his face and followed Beatrice as she got up and exited the dining room. They went back down the same hallway where the family art gallery was. Beatrice explained that to go to the main parts of the house, you exit the main doors of the dining room, to go outside to the courtyard or to class, you exit the side doors of the dining room, and if you wanted to go to the kitchen, you exit the back doors of the dining room. It didn't sound so complicated to him when she explained it that way.

"What's class?" Sebastian asked.

"Well, some days it's not necessarily my favorite thing, but we do get a chance to learn new things," Bea explained. "Mom and Dad make sure we have the best of the best when it comes to our education. We have class every day for four hours."

Sebastian didn't know if he was going to like class, but he had already deduced that in this house, it is just best if you go with the flow. As they headed down the art hallway, Sebastian started thinking about what kind of painting he would create. His mind started mixing colors, shapes, and ideas. It was so easy for him to get lost inside his mind. He had done it for many years, it had almost become a place of refuge for him. He thought of painting cars, gardens, or even little yellow flowers. He abruptly bumped into the back of Beatrice, who had stopped at the fifth door on the left.

"We are here," she whispered. "Class is a quiet place. No monkey business," she winked at Sebastian.

Beatrice opened the door and went inside. Sebastian was close in tow. This room was actually smaller than any of the other rooms inside the mansion. Three of the walls were painted a green that mirrored the lush St. Augustine in the garden. The final wall was the largest in the room and was painted black and was covered in chalk writing. Sebastian couldn't make out any of the words, but he knew they were letters and numbers. There was an oversized desk in front of that wall. It was very organized with papers, office supplies, and a single apple on it. Around the room were several different posters. Sebastian saw animals, maps, numbers, letters, shapes, colors, and other educational material. On one of the green walls, there were multiple papers that had been pinned to it. Each had a star sticker in the top right-hand corner. Bea caught Sebastian looking at them and she pointed to herself and smiled. Sebastian assumed those must be her papers, and a star sticker must mean something good. He wanted a star sticker! Bea had slipped into one of the two small desks that were sitting in the center of the room in front of the large desk with the apple. The frames of the small desks were wrought iron like the gazebo. Each desk had a small rectangle wooden box that was hinged in the back and opened. On the top of each box was a thin line that had been carved into the wooden box and it housed a single pencil. Beatrice opened her desk, grabbed a sheet of paper and began writing. Sebastian tried to mimic what she was doing, so he slipped into the other desk of the pair and got a piece of paper and began scribbling on it. He watched as Beatrice seemed engrossed in what she was doing. Sebastian peeked over to her paper and realized she was writing the things that were on the black wall behind the large desk. Hers looked even better than the board. He was impressed. If he had a star, he would give it to her. He looked back at the tiny scribbles on his paper. He let out a heavy sigh. He didn't think he would ever be getting a star sticker. Beatrice poked his shoulder with her pencil.

"Don't you worry bub, that is what the teacher is for. She will show you how to do everything," Beatrice encouraged.

"What's a teacher?" he asked.

"She will show you how to do things, tell you about the world, and help you to be very smart!" Bea cheered.

Realizing she had gotten too loud, she put her finger to her lips and went back to writing.

"Well, who is she?" Sebastian questioned.

"It's a surprise, but you will love her," Beatrice promised.

Almost as if she was called in, the teacher entered the room.

"Afternoon class, let's begin with our ABC's. Please repeat after me," instructed the lady.

She had her back to the children, but Sebastian was pretty sure he knew exactly who it was. Beatrice chuckled and began reciting each letter directly after the teacher. Sebastian began too. At the end of letters, the teacher went through shapes, colors, and numbers pointing to each thing she said on the black wall. When she had completed the repeating exercise, she finally turned around. Although she was wearing small wired-framed glasses, she still looked the same.

"Class, I am Ms. Grace. I have been and always will be your tutor. I expect yes ma'ams and good grades. I also expect you to allow your mind to soar as we learn new things."

"Nana," Sebastian shouted out.

"Uh-uh-uh, raise your hand please, if you wish to speak," Nana Grace commanded as she winked at Sebastian. "I take education very seriously. Please finish your writings, turn them into my desk, and then we will begin our lessons. Today, we are traveling to Africa and learning about its beginning, people, and animals."

With that, she sat at her desk and began going over her own papers. Sebastian wondered how she had the time to fit in teaching them every day. He was actually relieved that it was Nana. He wasn't sure he could deal with any more changes.

The next four hours, Nana went over Africa in detail. Nana had pictures, models, and videos. She made animal noises, jumped on the desk, and even ran around the room imitating a dazzle of zebras roaming the Savannahs. She explained how the world had seven continents, and Africa was the second largest. She covered every bit of information she could fit into those four hours. Sebastian was in complete awe. He sat on the edge of his seat the entire time. He had no idea the world was so big or that Nana knew so much.

"Ok class," Nana said out of breath, "that will complete today's lesson."

She had just finished doing a traditional African dance. She had tried coaxing Sebastian to join her, but he had declined.

Today he had already sung a silly tune with Bea, was the champion of his first fork fight, and attended class. He figured that was plenty of new experiences for one day, he wasn't sure he could do another. Bea however did not hesitate when it was her turn to join. She jumped out of her desk, let out a high-pitched squeal, and danced her heart out. Sebastian watched in amusement. Nana and Bea circled the room in unison with their synchronized steps. Sebastian couldn't believe that Bea had picked up on the dance so quickly. She was a natural. He also couldn't believe that Nana had so much pep in her. Her roundness had not gotten in the way of her dancing skills. Nana even had a djembe. She let Beatrice keep dancing while she kept an upbeat rhythm with it that accompanied the cd she was playing. She offered Sebastian a chance to play. Although he had turned down the dancing, he really wanted to try this. He had never seen an instrument before, but it looked easy enough, plus he was able to stay at his desk and play. For the last several minutes of class, he beat the djembe and Beatrice and Nana danced around the room. He hoped that every class was going to be as exciting as this one. He knew, with Nana as his teacher, he was going to be very smart, and he would get his very own star sticker. He didn't know what all she would teach, but he was now looking forward to their daily classes. Even though Mr. and Mrs. weren't there, and hadn't been for a while, Sebastian thanked them in his mind for taking him in and already giving him so much. He wished they were there, he enjoyed them being around, but he had Beatrice. He was her bub, and he was content. As long as he had her, he knew his life would be full and happy. At the beginning of class, Nana had given each of the children a sheet that had the shape of Africa on it to color. She had written his name on the paper, and it was the first time Sebastian had ever seen it before. She told him she wrote in cursive, and that very soon she would teach him how to do it himself. Nana instructed the children to finish the sheet, clean up, turn their papers in to be graded and head off to play because class was over. Sebastian was almost sad; class had gone by so fast and he wasn't really ready for it to be over.

"Hurry, bub, I can't wait to play outside with you," Bea exclaimed! She jumped up, turned her paper in, and bolted for the door. "Don't forget, just straight down the hall to the glass doors. I will be waiting for you on the swings," Bea instructed Sebastian.

Sebastian was doing his best to make sure his sheet was nicely done. He hadn't ever colored before but didn't want to tell Nana or Bea that out of embarrassment. He realized there was probably a lot in life he hadn't ever done. A slight instance of anger flashed inside of him towards his momma from keeping him from these experiences. It quickly disseminated when Nana came and placed her hand on his shoulder.

"Are you done, dear?" she questioned.

He picked up his blue crayon and finished the bottom tip of Africa and shook his head yes. She grabbed it from him and put it on her desk. He gathered his items and slowly headed for the door. He smiled to himself, he had finished his first paper on his first day of class. He felt proud of himself.

"Ahem, Sebastian," Nana cleared her throat.

His pride quickly vanished; he couldn't believe he had already messed up. He already had one hand on the door and wished he would have moved a little faster. He slowly turned to see what he had done wrong. As he turned around, he saw Nana walking to the wall where Bea's papers almost covered it. Right on top, Nana pinned his paper.

"Very good job, my dear. It was excellent work," she bragged.

Sebastian stared at the paper in disbelief. At the very top right-hand corner, was a shiny gold star. He blurted out a quick 'thank you' and a small squeal and ran down the hall to the garden to tell Bea the good news.

Chapter 7: Disappointment

Sebastian's next three and a half years of life flew by. He adored Beatrice and the pair were inseparable and unstoppable. They had settled into a satisfying routine. Every morning they met in Bea's room. They would go into their private library and get lost in books. Thanks to Ms. Grace, Sebastian was already an accelerated reader. He had breezed past the letters in the alphabet, tackled long and short sounds, and easily aced blends. He was a natural reader. They would each grab the book they were in the middle of, read for about 15 minutes, switch books with each other, and read another 15 minutes. When time was up, they would discuss the books they had read. Oftentimes, depending on the content, they usually wound up acting out the book. They had been pirates, dragons, dogs and a slew of other characters. This was their favorite way to start the day. By 9:00 prompt, they were downstairs in the dining room at the table waiting for Nana to bring them breakfast. They had learned the importance of punctuality about a year ago. It was a hard, but great, life lesson. One morning, they began their routine as usual, but they got completely lost in their book adventures. On that particular morning, they were reading books about space and cowboys. After their discussion, Sebastian climbed onto the sofa, whipped his good arm around his head like a lasso and bellowed out a very loud *yee-haw*. Not to be outdone by her kid brother, Bea stood on the sofa right next to him, altered her voice, and coldly said, "Houston, we have a problem." The two burst out laughing, and this started the most epic game of space cowboys anyone had ever played. Sebastian and Beatrice, because of the amount of time they spent with each other, had developed quite an imagination. Any situation in life could turn into an adventure with them. Mr. and Mrs. were hardly every home, and although the children secretly despised this, they took comfort in each other. During their space cowboy game, they lost track of time. They knew breakfast was served at 9:00, and they could each tell time, but they were enthralled in the game they were playing. When that large grandfather clock struck 9, they didn't even notice. However, about an hour later, they did notice when Nana Grace started hollering through the secret door.

"Children, you better get down these stairs right now!"

Both children looked at each other with widening eyes. They knew they were in for it. They raced down the stairs and into their seats, waiting for Nana to come out. It seemed like eternity that they were sitting at that table. The sound in her voice resonated her frustration and disappointment. When she did emerge from the kitchen, she had two carts. The first was full of the usual breakfast delights. She had spared no effort on their breakfast. Every breakfast meat and every baked good was on the cart. As usual, it all looked like it was cooked to perfection. The kid's stomachs grumbled simultaneously; they didn't realize they were that hungry. The second cart was not as appeasing. It housed two single bowls of oats. They didn't have brown sugar, fruit, or granola on them. They were just two sad blue bowls full of plain oats. Confused by the presentation, the children just sat there, not daring to question what Nana was doing. She picked up the two bowls and placed one in front of each child.

"Eat," she ordered.

The kids slowly picked up their spoon and took a bite. The two just thought the sight of those oats was awful, until they tasted them. They were cold and lacked any flavor. The children were actually surprised, Nana had never made anything that didn't taste good. After two bites, Bea put her spoon down, wiped her mouth, and rested back in her chair. She was determined she was done. Sebastian was secretly relieved she did it first, because he wanted to join suit. As he was putting his spoon down, Nana did another thing she had never done before. Nana came to the table and sat down in the chair directly across from Beatrice.

"Young lady, you will eat the entire bowl," she demanded.

Beatrice was in shock.

"Are you serious, Nana, I am sorry, but this does not taste good, and it's very cold," she whined.

"I don't care, if you two would have been mindful to be on time, your food wouldn't be cold. You both have the world at your disposal. I cook three meals a day for you, and then a snack whenever you desire. I clean your rooms and take care of your home. I double as your educator. I have never asked for anything from the two of you in return other than common courteousness. I expect you to say thank you, to be polite, and to appreciate all you have been given."

With that, she left the room wheeling the other cart back into the kitchen. She never raised her voice during the entire conversation. She was stern, but the children could still tell that she loved them very much.

"You know, Bea, I feel really lousy," Sebastian moaned.

"Ya, I know, it was really awful of us to make her wait like that," Beatrice added.

"She has been so nice to me since I moved in here four years ago, and I really should remember to show her how thankful I am. I don't want her to feel bad, or like I don't appreciate her. She is one of my favorite people in the whole world." Sebastian sniffled.

"Ya, bub, I know how you feel. She has been like a second mom to me. She has been with me for twelve years and has helped take care of me from day one. Heck, she actually does more for me than my own mom. Now, I feel really, really lousy too. I hate that we made her feel like we don't notice all the things she does for us," Beatrice started crying too.

Both children had tears streaming down their faces when Nana came back in the dining room. She came to the table and stood in between them both. She pulled two hankies from her white gloved hands and dabbed both of their faces.

"Nana, we are so sorry," both children wailed in unison.

"We do love you so much," Beatrice assured.

"You have been so good to me and I thank you," Sebastian complemented.

Both children laid over on Nana and continued to sob. They nestled their heads into her plump belly and bellowed louder.

"There, there my dears," she cooed while she patted their heads. "I know you do, and I love you both to the moon and back. Just be mindful of the ones who care for you. Try not to ever take that for granted. Now hush up those tears, because your Nana already forgave you both," she coddled.

Both children sucked up their tears and blew their noses in the tissues from Nana. They sat back up in their chairs. Nana started heading back out the kitchen.

"About those oats, you must still eat them all. Nothing about that has changed. We wouldn't want to be wasteful of our provisions, now would we?"

With those words of wisdom, she dashed back into the kitchen one last time. The children didn't dare argue and they both spent the next ten minutes in silence finishing their now brunch. When they finished, they even put their own bowls in the sink.

Even though that was a year ago, both children knew that Nana had taught them an important life lesson they would never forget. Now sitting at breakfast enjoying a wonderful meal of chocolate crepes and fresh fruit, the children laughed and joked. It was a distant memory, but it forever changed the way they treated their dear Nana. After breakfast, the children headed to music class. Nana had added this course to their curriculum two years ago. Beatrice was being instructed on the piano, and Sebastian was learning the violin. They had learned so quickly and were very advanced in their playing. They were both exquisite on their respective instruments, and during music hour the house echoed with the sounds of Beethoven, Bach, Strauss, and Chopin. It was breathtaking to listen to. You would think that two children would be in stiff competition with each other. However, these two complemented each other beautifully. Their playing mirrored their life, pure harmony. Music class lasted two hours and was scheduled before their normal classes. Over the last four years, Ms. Grace had vastly expanded their minds. She had taken them to parts of the country Sebastian never knew existed. They had even done science experiments where they blew stuff up. Sebastian least favorite classes were Mathematics and Grammar. Even though he didn't like them, he was still very good at both subjects. Nana often commented that he must have a brain two sizes bigger than his head. He had since surpassed Beatrice's gold star collection, but she didn't seem to mind. She didn't seem to care about class ever. At twelve years old, she rarely paid attention. Sebastian had even caught her sleeping from time to time. He didn't understand this about his sister. He couldn't get enough of class, even the subjects he didn't really like. He loved how he could go to an alternate life through learning. When Ms. Grace taught, he really felt like she was taking him to another dimension and he was living the information she was teaching. It thrilled him. He tried explaining this to Bea, but she never really understood. Today's lesson ended much sooner than usual.

"Ok class, I have a great surprise. Your mother and father are coming home today. I know you haven't seen them much in the last four years. They missed both of your birthdays and Christmas last year, but they found some time to get away and are taking advantage of it. They will be here in about two hours, so we are wrapping class up early, so you can both get showers and put on your best clothes for them. Now, Sebastian, I know you love that striped purple shirt and those khaki shorts, but today, please put on something a little dressier," Nana begged.

Both children squealed in excitement and hugged each other. They hadn't realized that Mr. and Mrs. had missed so much last year until Nana pointed it out, and they were both super excited to see them. Sebastian had grown very fond of the couple over the last four years. He could only count on two hands and two feet how many times he had seen them during his forever placement, but when they were there, they were incredible. They always had prizes for the children when they came home. They played with them, took them places, and doted on them both. They were excellent at giving each of the children attention while they were together and still finding a way to make each child feel unique and special to them. Sebastian sometimes struggled with calling Mrs. "mom"; he felt a small sting of betrayal course through his body when he said it. He had no problem calling Mr. "dad." He loved that he had a dad. He had never had a father before, and he adored the relationship they had. When dad was away, Sebastian was the man of the house and he took that responsibility seriously. He wanted to make his dad proud, and he took personal pride in the idea of keeping Bea safe. His dad continued to call him Bud, and it was one of the things he looked forward to most when they were coming home, because he didn't get to hear it very often. He didn't like that they were always gone, so when they came home, the children soaked in every minute of their time. Since they were usually only back for maybe a week at a time, all classes stopped while they were in town. They didn't want to waste a minute of their time doing anything else when mom and dad were home. Both children jumped down from their desks, hugged Nana, and headed to their rooms to get ready for their parents. They knew they had two hours to get ready and they wanted to make sure they were perfect. They chased each other up the stairs. Reaching the top, they were completely out of breath.

"Ok, let's meet back here at your door," Bea gasped.

"Then we will walk down together to see mom and dad," Sebastian huffed.

"Couldn't have said it better myself," Bea replied with a wink.

The two hugged again and went into their separate rooms to get ready.

Within forty-five minutes, Sebastian was ready. When he was bathing, he took extra care to make sure and clean really well. Usually he didn't care that much about his hygiene and would mainly just stand under the water. Nana always knew though. She would have him go right back into his bathroom and re-wash. She told him he might as well do it right the first time, because she would always know. He had tried over the last four years to get away with it, but Nana had a nose like a bloodhound. In his mind, it had become their little game. He hadn't seen Mr. and Mrs. in so long, he wanted to make sure he was perfect. He opened his closet and looked at his wardrobe. He smiled at the sight of it. He definitely had a unique sense of style. The first outfit he ever wore in his new home was so special, he hadn't wanted to wear anything else. For weeks, he begged Nana to keep washing it, so he could wear it the next day. Nana had surprised him a month into his stay with a closet full of clothes. She took the same dark purple and light purple striped pattern he loved and had the tailor make him pieces in the same print. He had long sleeve shirts, short sleeve shirts, tank tops, jackets, button down shirts and even suit jackets. He loved his khaki shorts as well. He had a closet full of khaki shorts, khaki pants, and even only khaki colored suit pants. At first, it seemed a little odd that he wore only the same print. He loved it. Nana said as long as he was wearing clean clothes and was happy, it was fine by her. The only thing he had that wasn't in that print were his white undershirts and his navy silk jammies. He pulled a pair of khaki pants, a white undershirt, and a purple striped suit jacket. He slipped on a pair of brown dress shoes. He brushed his teeth and combed his hair. He spent extra-long on his hair trying to make the part perfect. He stepped back, looked in the mirror, and was satisfied with what he saw. He smiled, displaying his missing front tooth which made him grin even wider. He looked perfect and knew Mr. and Mrs. would be pleased. He couldn't wait to show Beatrice how good he looked. Four doors down, Beatrice was also taking special care to get ready. She took a long hot bath. She always made sure she was clean. She had never liked feeling icky. Her closet told a different story. It was full of a rainbow of colors. There were many different textiles that included lace, tulle, silk, and chiffon. The only thing that was the same, were they were all princess style dresses. She loved feeling like a princess. Her favorite color was pink, and she had her eye on a baby pink tulle skirted dress, but she knew her mom loved blue. She grabbed a pale blue chiffon dress and held it up to herself in the mirror. It was gorgeous. She knew her mom would love it. She added her sparkly black dress shoes. She braided her hair into two French braids and put a black bow at the end of each braid. This was her dad's favorite way for her to wear her hair. After she put the dress on, she twirled twice. This was one of her best spinning dresses. She opened her dresser drawer and pulled out a blue bow tie. She went to Mr. Bunny's cage and called him to her. She explained to him that mom and dad were coming home, and she placed the bow tie around his neck. She wanted to make sure everyone looked their best. She looked at her clock and she was right on time. She grabbed Mr. Bunny, tucked him under her arm and hurried out the door. She nearly knocked over Sebastian, who had his hand lifted to knock on her door.

"Wow, Bea, you look just like a pretty princess," Sebastian gushed.

"Shucks, bub, you look really handsome too!" she replied.

They grabbed each other's hands and headed down the stairs. Down the stairs, they both almost knocked over Nana.

"Easy does it, my dears, you nearly knocked me on my caboose," Nana chuckled.

"Sorry, Nana, we are just so excited to see Mom and Dad," Bea exclaimed.

"I understand, it's no problem. They should be here any minute, so why don't you both go wait on the window seat in the foyer," Nana suggested.

The children didn't hesitate and raced to the window seat. They both climbed on it and pulled back the deep burgundy curtain to peek out the window together. They couldn't believe their parents would actually be home again. They really couldn't remember the last time it had been. They started discussing when they thought it was. They finally concluded that it had been four months previous, around Easter. They remembered because they all went to church together, as a family, for Easter services. They had discussed it for about twenty minutes and still had seen no sign of them. They decided to find other ways to kill the time, assuming their parent's flight may have been delayed. The finished eye-spy, twenty questions, and "I'm going on a bear hunt" and still no sign of them. Bea did her best to occupy their time, but Sebastian could tell that she was getting worried that she hadn't heard from them. She didn't say this to Sebastian, but he knew her well enough. Every time she was worried, she would flip her hair twice. Depending on how she was wearing her hair for the day would determine which direction she flipped it first. It never failed, there were always two flips. She did her best to hide it, and most probably didn't even realize that about her, but he knew. In true Bea form, she peered out the window again, and then flipped her braid, once to the front, and then back again. She was worried. Within seconds of her hair flip, Beatrice suggested she should go check in with Nana, but Sebastian should stand guard and holler if they showed up. Agreeing to the plan, Sebastian turned back to peer into the window. As Beatrice and Mr. Bunny skipped off, Sebastian put his head in his hands.

He was starting to get upset. He could feel his temper rising. Why would they not have called if their plane was delayed? Didn't they know how much everyone would worry when they were late? Didn't they know how upset Bea would be if they didn't call? He could handle all the worry, but his sister was fragile. She shouldn't have to worry like this. They would know that if they were around more, if they were there for her like she was. At this point, he was so angry he didn't even care to watch for them anymore. How could they do this to Bea? His Bea. He turned from the window and folded his arms across his chest. They were now an hour and a half late; he sure hoped they had called Nana. It was, of course, the polite thing to do. He was about to go off again on Mr. and Mrs. in his head, when Bea came back around the corner. She saw him with his arms folded and a puzzled look shot across her face. He realized he still had his arms folded, and quickly dropped them to his side.

"What's wrong, Bub," she questioned. "They haven't called yet, but they will be here, I just know they will. They wouldn't let us down like that. They know how much we miss them, and I know they miss us too. Just a little longer."

She came back to the window seat and patted his back. He instantly felt better and didn't want to do anything to upset his sister, so he turned back around with her. After another thirty minutes, they still hadn't heard anything.

"Mr. Bunny is getting restless," Bea stated. "He has been so good, but I think he needs a nap. I am going to run him back upstairs. Keep guard, I will be right back."

Sebastian nodded and continued staring outside. At this point, he was just doing it to make Bea happy; but he had already deduced that they weren't coming. He wasn't sure how Bea couldn't see it. Before she even had a chance to come back, Nana came into the foyer.

"Sebastian, dear, where is your sister?" she questioned sadly.

When he turned, her face confirmed his beliefs. They weren't coming, his anger flared up again.

"I am here, Nana," Bea gleaned.

"Children, please remember your parents love you very much. Their work is just very important. They save lives," Nana exclaimed.

Bea had started running down the stairs, but after hearing this, she stopped dead in her tracks.

"What are you saying?" Bea quivered.

"Here, there is a call for you both," she said as she handed Sebastian the phone.

He waited for Bea to get to him and he put the phone up to both of their ears. He refused to speak.

"Hello," Bea said shakily.

"Hey, Bud, hey, Sport! Listen, we miss you guys so very much. We were on our way home for a few days. Our plane actually touched down, when we were called back in. One of our new chemicals that we created had an adverse effect on a patient and sent them into anaphylactic shock. It was just awful," Mr. explained.

"They don't know what that is dear," Mrs. said in the background.

"Oh right, right, it means they didn't respond like we thought they would, and their face started swelling. It could keep them from breathing," Mr. further explained. "We had to get back, because the treatment was supposed to solve their condition, but we have to make sure it hasn't actually made it worse. If our working is hindering instead of helping, you don't want to know what the govern;

"That's too much information, honey" Mrs. interrupted, again in the background. "They are coming, honey, we have to go. Tell the children how much we love them and wish we could be there with them, and that we will come home as soon as we can."

"Your mother is right, we love you two more than you can know, even though it seems like we are never there, we are always in your hearts," Mr. assured.

Beatrice swallowed hard, fighting the tears. "Yea, we understand, Dad, we are both here, and we love you. Go help people, we know it is important work and we are proud of you," Bea managed to say without losing it.

"Thanks honey, you two are the best. Be good for Nana, work hard on your lessons. Love you both." With that, Mr. disconnected the line.

Beatrice dropped the phone to the ground and ran back up the stairs. Nana reached down to grab the phone and told Sebastian she would go check in on her.

"I got it, don't worry, Nana, you can start dinner," Sebastian offered.

"Take your time, dears, this time being a little late won't be a problem," Nana sweetly said and then kissed Sebastian on the forehead.

He closed his eyes, trying to hold back his own tears. He shook the pain away, focused on helping Beatrice. He sprinted up the stairs and burst into her room. He didn't see her in the main part of her room or her bathroom. Mr. Bunny was on the top floor of his cage eating a freshly prepared salad. So, if she wasn't on her bed, or with Mr. Bunny, she could only be in one place. He ran to her closet and belly crawled through the secret door. Halfway through the secret entrance, he heard his suit coat rip. Annoyed by this, he huffed out loud. This was their parent's fault. He loved that jacket. He shook that thought out of his head too. He knew Nana would sew it back up for him. He made it through to the other side and jumped up. He saw her. She was sitting on the sofa with her back to the door. She had her knees to her chest and her head buried in them. Her body was shaking, and Sebastian could hear her sobbing. It was almost more than he could handle.

"Bea, please don't cry," Sebastian softly said.

He ran to her and sat behind her. He patted her back, mimicking what she had just done for him earlier in the foyer.

"You know it is important work, you said so yourself," he tried.

"We are important too," she sniffled, wiping the snot from her nose. "They should have come back this time. They should have known how much I needed them too," she continued.

"I know, it doesn't seem fair," Sebastian offered. "But hey, we have each other, remember? We belong together. That is enough. Let's go do something. Let's go see Mr. Bunny and give him a treat, you love that," he tried.

Beatrice placed her head back down on her knees, but she wasn't crying as hard now.

"How about we go have Nana whip us up some ice cream sundaes. I will even let you have my cherry," he tempted.

She just sighed.

"Let's read your favorite book. The one about the knight and the princess," he said excitedly.

She didn't even move a muscle.

"Ok, I got it, let's go to the garden and swing. I will push you the whole time," he tried again.

She just shook her head. He got in front of her determined to make her smile. He sang silly songs, did silly dances, and made silly faces. As hard as he tried, nothing seemed to get through to her. It was not usually this hard to turn her spirits around. He sat in front of her and she turned her head. He could feel his anger rising again. He took a deep breath in and released it. He did this three times; he didn't want her to see him angry. What else could he do? Finally, it hit him. He had no idea why he hadn't thought of it before now. It should have been the very first thing he tried. If this didn't work, she would need an intervention. No matter what, this always did the trick. If Bea was sad, depressed, or angry, even if it was at Sebastian, this always worked. He jumped to his feet, cleared his throat, and tapped her on the shoulder twice. She turned her head towards him. Tears stained her cheeks. Her once perfectly braided hair was now a mess.

"Sebastian, I think I just need to," she began.

Sebastian didn't let her finish her thought.

"You wanna play our favorite game?" he questioned with a smirk on his face.

Chapter 8: Forbidden

"Well, what do you say?" he questioned.

He held his breath as he waited for her response. He needed this to work, he needed his sister to be happy again.

"Fine," she said as she jumped up, "but you have to be the fox first," she demanded.

"It's a deal," Sebastian complied.

He watched as she undid both of her braids and shook her hair out. She slipped her shoes off and stuffed them under the couch.

"Have you done anything to set it up?" she asked.

"Not yet, but I promise I will take care of everything. You gotta give me like ten minutes though," Sebastian assured.

"Yea take your time, I am going to put on my nightgown anyways. It will be easier to play in than this dress," she stated.

"Ok, that is perfect, I will meet you in your room as soon as it is all set up," Sebastian informed.

He wiggled back through the secret door with Bea close in tow. He walked through the closet and headed to the door to go get set up. As he was exiting, Beatrice stopped him. "You're the best, Bub, thanks," she said as she flashed him her famous Bea smile.

He quickly smiled back and darted out the door, elated his plan had worked. It normally always took him more than ten minutes to set up "foxes and bloodhounds" but he didn't want to risk giving Bea too much time to think about everything that had just happened with their parents. He was happy that he always kept a few hiding spots and clues in his arsenal for this game, so he was pretty much ready to go anytime Beatrice felt like playing. This was their favorite game, but they always seemed to get into some trouble when they played, so they only brought it out on special occasions. They had broken two table lamps, knocked a painting off the wall in the family gallery, which when it landed on the floor, the glass in the frame shattered into a million pieces, and they had managed to rip one of the chairs in the dining room. The chair bothered Nana the most, since a replacement chair had to be custom ordered and as Nana said, "cost a pretty penny." Sebastian was sure Nana was off on her math and those chairs cost quite a bit more than a penny. In fact, her irate reaction hadn't made sense to Sebastian. If the chair only cost a penny, he knew he could find one of those laying around the house. Beatrice had to explain to him that she was just using an expression, and the chair was quite expensive. It was usually Beatrice's fault that the game became destructive, she was a little reckless when they played. Sebastian had taken the heat for the chair, and she had later knighted him Sir Sebastian for his chivalry. The duo played many games together, but they had both agreed that this was their favorite. They had invented this game, so it made it special. The rules seemed complex at first, but it was actually a very simple game to play. One person was a fox and the other was the bloodhound. It was a modified hide-and-seek, tag, and scavenger hunt game. The main fox got to hide three mini-foxes anywhere in the house. The only stipulation was that it had to be in plain sight. The items that were used as mini-foxes changed all the time. Tonight, the mini-foxes were Mr. Bunny's rabbit treats. Sebastian figured after the round was over, they could feed them to Mr. Bunny. He knew she had turned the idea down moments ago, but he was hoping after the game, she would be excited to do it. Once the bloodhound found all three mini-foxes, she had to find the main fox, which, in this case, was Sebastian. With each mini-fox, two clues were left to where the main fox would be hiding. The trick was, the main fox could move between the two different hiding spots as many times as they wanted, if they chose to, making it harder to be found. If the bloodhound caught the fox mid-move, then the game was over. The bloodhound couldn't actively seek the fox until all the mini-foxes were found. The fox also had to be very stealthy in moving as to not to get caught. It was almost as if both the fox and bloodhound were playing hide and seek from each other. The reason things normally got broken was when Bea would find the mini-foxes, she was not very delicate in her retrieval. She also had a tendency of breaking things when she spotted the main fox moving and would chase him down to tag him. Sebastian stopped in the kitchen to let Nana know they were going to play their favorite game, so they may be later to dinner than she was expecting. He could see her look of disapproval as she twisted her face in disgust.

"Oh, you know I hate that game," she groaned.

Sebastian looked at her as pitiful as he could.

"Honest, Nana, it was the only thing that put a smile on Bea's face. We will be careful this time," Sebastian promised.

"Well I don't believe that for a second, but if it will keep a smile on both of your dear faces, I can't argue with it. I will finish dinner and leave you two plates on the table, covered. I think I am going to turn in if it gets too late, so just be a big help and put your plates in the kitchen when you are through if you don't see me," she instructed.

"You got it, Nana, that will be no problem at all," Sebastian assured.

He ran out of the kitchen, stopping to put a treat and clues on the dining room table. Clue #1a-You can find me high. Clue #1b-You can find me low. He had decided his two hiding spots would be their upstairs library and the downstairs guest bathroom. He wanted to leave vague clues, but he also didn't want

Bea to get discouraged. He didn't feel he was necessarily cheating for her, but merely assuring she would have fun, but still find him in the end. He sprinted to the front foyer and left another treat on the mantle of the fireplace. Clue #2a-You can find me from a to z. Clue #2b-You need me for one to two. He ran to the schoolroom and left the last treat on Mrs. Grace's desk. Clue #3a-Easily our favorite place in the house. Clue#3b-I am mainly used for the guests, and we each have one in our bedrooms. He was satisfied with his quick clues. He ran back to Bea's bedroom to see if she was ready. When he got there, she was sitting on her bed brushing out her hair. When she saw him, she jumped up, clearly eager to play.

"Ok, it is all set up. You know the rules, I need five minutes to get into place," Sebastian reminded.

"Sebastian, you also know the rules, you can't go outside, and you can't hide in the lab, it is forbidden," Beatrice ordered.

"I know, I know," Sebastian said.

Without another word, he ran out of Beatrice's room. She looked up at the clock on her wall, waiting for her five-minute timer to end. She didn't even wait an extra second, as soon as five minutes hit, she raced out the door. The excitement of the game rushed over her. She searched Sebastian's room looking for her mini-foxes. With no luck, she made her way down the staircase and towards the dining room. Sebastian could hear her footsteps and laughter ringing through the house as he hid behind the shower curtain in the guest bath. He had left the light off, and the door cracked so he would know when he had time to make his escape upstairs. He knew he wanted to be found in their library, because he wanted to surround Beatrice in all her favorite things to make sure her spirits stayed lifted. She ran past the bathroom door. She was calling out his name, even though she knew he wouldn't answer. He heard her open the dining room doors, but he knew he wouldn't have enough time to get out of the bath because she would see the treat quickly. He did have enough time to move out of the tub and behind the door.

"Ha, Mr. Bunny's treats are the mini-foxes," she hollered out. "I love it!"

He knew it was a good idea.

"Ok, Bub, so those clues basically tell me you are upstairs or downstairs, very helpful," she teased.

He could feel the smile spread across his face. This is exactly what she needed. He needed it too. He was upset about his parents, but he could handle it. He could no longer hear her laughing, so he assumed she was making it down the back hallway towards the family gallery and school room and he knew this was his chance to try and make it upstairs. He made a fervent dash to the main stairway. He tripped on the third stair and landed with a thud. Afraid his cover was blown, he lay still for a moment. He still couldn't hear her, so he got up and continued up the staircase. As he neared the main landing, he could hear her laughter coming back through the dining room. He could feel the sweat running down his neck and he picked up his pace. He knew if she came through those doors before he got up the stairs she would see him, and then tag would ensue. He reached the very top of the staircase and knew he needed to make it to her bedroom. The last clue was downstairs, so as long as he could get to her room, he would be fine and could just patiently wait for her to find him.

"Ok, I think I know where one of your hiding spots is, but I still need a mini-fox," she called out.

She didn't know which spot he was in, so she was yelling as loud as she could to make sure he would hear her. He was pressed up against the first door on the top of the stairs. He needed to make it three more doors down and across the hall before she got to the final clue on the mantle and made her way to him. He wasn't prepared for what she did next.

"Sebastian, I have to go to the restroom, and I am going to use mine, so just stay where you are, but we are going to do a brief time out," she rang out.

This was not part of the plan. If she came up the stairs and saw him, he would have nowhere to go. Now, he wouldn't make it to her room, especially if that is where she was going. He sprinted down the hall past her door. He tried to get into the next two rooms and they were both locked. He could hear her singing as she ascended the stairs. He could tell she was only walking; she was probably out of breath from running around looking for clues. This was his only saving grace. He tried the next four doors in the hall and they were all locked.

Why did Nana have to keep them all locked? he groaned to himself.

He was nearing the end of the hall and knew he would just have to wait on the stairs. He wasn't supposed to even be this far down the hall, but he had no choice. He rounded the corner and went two stairs up and waited. It wasn't a second too soon, because he could now hear Beatrice on the main floor. He waited to see if he had been spotted. She never stopped singing. He heard her at the end of the hall, a door open, her singing muffle, and a door shut. He knew she had gone into her room. He wiped the sweat from his forehead. That was too close. He felt a chill run down his spine. It reminded him that he was standing on the forbidden staircase. He was shown this staircase within the first month of being there. At the end of their hall on the right was another staircase in the mansion. It led to the third floor. The only thing on the third floor was the lab. He had been told a million times he wasn't allowed in there, let alone on the staircase. The lab was always to remain locked, and nobody was to go in there because their parents work was top secret. They had even gone as far as to ask the children if they wanted to be responsible for the death of innocent people. Of course, the children had said no, shaking in fear, not realizing this was just a scare tactic. Standing on the stairwell now, he had a sick feeling in his stomach. He wanted nothing more to get away from these stairs. He was happy to never go near the staircase again. While he was trying to will Beatrice to hurry up in his mind, he heard something coming from above him. He figured it was just in his head and redirected his attention back to listening for Beatrice's exit. He heard another noise from above and this time knew it wasn't just in his mind. An unsettling thought crossed his mind, and he felt his temper flaring up again. Were his parents secretly home? Had they come back to get something from their precious lab and hadn't bothered to even say hello to their children? The more he thought about this, his anger intensified. This was the last straw. They needed to know what they were doing to Beatrice. He glanced down the hall towards Bea's room. Her door was still closed, but her light was on. He knew she was still in there. She probably got side-tracked with Mr. Bunny. That was so like her. He decided he would just sneak up to the lab, tell them off, and be back in time to finish the game with Beatrice. Clearly, they didn't want the kids to know they were home, so he knew they probably wouldn't make a big deal about him going up there tonight. If they did, they would risk Beatrice finding out how they had betrayed her. He wouldn't tell her either, he couldn't bear to see her upset by it. He tiptoed up the stairs quietly, planning exactly what he wanted to say to them. He wasn't going to hold back. They were grown adults, surely, they had to know how their job affected him and Beatrice.

He was now thankful that he had spent his years as a tyke with cats. When he took his time and concentrated, he had picked up their cat-like maneuvers. As he climbed up this stair-case, there was no chance of him tripping like he had done at the start of their game. He scaled each stair delicately. He didn't want to risk being heard early; he wanted the shock factor. He couldn't wait to see the looks on his parent's face, when he unraveled their selfish secret. He continued up the stairs, not realizing the staircase was so large. Beatrice entered his mind, and he wondered where she was in the game. He knew she would continue searching after she figured out his two hiding spots. Since they were allowed to move multiple times in the game, he figured she would assume he was putting his stealth to good use and going back and forth. Still, he didn't want to spend too much time chewing out his parents, he wanted to make sure he got back to Bea quickly. He had successfully climbed ten more stairs without being noticed and he could hear voices. He could finally see the top of the stairs, where an unsettling yellow glow filled the landing. The voices were hushed so he couldn't tell what was being said, but he had deduced it was Mrs. because he could tell the voice was female. This part of the mansion didn't feel like the rest of it. When he reached the landing, he realized he was in a tower of the mansion. He knew it had multiple towers, but he thought they were all for show. Everything was dark, except the crack under the door of the lab, so he couldn't make out in great detail how this area of the mansion was decorated. To the left of the entrance to the staircase was a single window. It wasn't very large, and didn't allow for much light to come in. It was adorned in drapes, which Sebastian assumed would be deep burgundy in color to match the rest of the house. As he approached the door for his surprise attack, Nana's voice stopped him. She was the voice in the lab. What was she doing in there? She was a part of the "nobody" who was allowed in there. He had heard his parents telling her the same rule. Now curiosity was getting the best of him. The door was cracked, so he stuck his ear as close to the door as he could get. Her voice kept fading in and out; Sebastian assumed she was walking around. He couldn't make out the entire conversation, but it seemed Nana was upset with whoever she was talking to. He never heard a response, so he made the conclusion she was on the phone. He listened to bits and pieces of what appeared to be a rant for about five minutes. He had heard enough to realize Nana was on the phone with their parents. She was angry that they hadn't come home to see the children. She was also creeped out to be in their lab. They asked her to retrieve some information in a filing cabinet and read it to them. He couldn't make out what she was reading, most of the words he had never heard before. He was shocked by this since Mrs. Grace was very thorough in her teaching. She also told them she had knocked over one of the chairs, which in turn knocked over some lab equipment which she refused to clean. That must have been the noise he had heard downstairs. Sebastian knew Nana had a bold side to her, but he was shocked she was speaking to them this way. He was secretly pleased that someone was giving them a piece of their mind since that was his original plan. Curiosity was getting the best of him again and he really wanted to know what was so important they allowed Nana to break their number one rule in the home. He wanted to see inside the lab. He wanted to understand what kept his parents away. He thought down to Beatrice, deduced he had only been gone about ten minutes, and reasoned that he could afford another ten minutes snooping around and then be back to the game and Bea would be none the wiser. He wanted to do this for her too, after all. He was mulling over a quick plan to sneak in without Nana seeing him when he heard her disconnect the phone. He heard heavy footsteps coming his way. Oh no, she was leaving. He panicked and dashed behind the curtain in the window. With his back to the curtain, he was now facing the lone window on this floor of the mansion. As his eyes adjusted to the moonlight, he realized he could oversee the entire front part of the property. There were three cars parked in front of the home. The landscaping looked perfect, even at night. He sighed; the house seemed picture perfect. Nobody would ever guess the hurt that was inside. He could hear Nana breathing heavily, she was now outside the lab. He slowed his own breathing and froze every muscle in his body. Great, now he wouldn't be able to snoop around the lab. Oh well, at least he would get back to Bea sooner.

"Ok, ole gal, pull yourself together now. I know you are upset but you must remember this stupid code to lock the lab. I know you wrote it down somewhere. Oh, here it is on your hand," a quiet voice said.

Relieved, Sebastian realized Nana was talking to herself.

"Oh, that's just the bee's knees," she said sarcastically. "My sweat smudged the numbers. Ok, that's 6-4, I think 1, 2. No, that didn't work."

Sebastian smirked; Nana would accidentally give him exactly what he needed to snoop in the lab. This couldn't have worked out more perfectly. He just had to remain motionless, so he didn't get caught. He could hear her trying other combinations. She said each one out loud, and he could hear her frustration rising.

"6,4,7,2, oh finally. I should have known. That is each month of each family member's birthdays, clever clever," she mused as she headed down the stairs.

Sebastian couldn't hear her steps, but he could still hear her talking to herself. As her voice faded, Sebastian peeked out behind the curtain. The same yellow glow was still coming from beneath the door. He went reluctantly to the door and stood there. He wasn't certain what he would find on the other side. He was committed to his plan and slowly entered the four-digit code. He could hear the lock click in compliance. He slowly pushed the door open. He was amazed when he stepped inside.

He closed the door behind him and inhaled deeply. This place was incredible. First, it was massive. This lab was easily the size of their library. Everything was intricately placed, except for the chair that was toppled over and the broken glass. That was Nana's handy work, no doubt. In the center of the room was a large table. On it sat various sized flasks filled with various colored liquids. Two main tubes ran above them. Splitting off the tubes were two mini tubes that ran into each flask. One appeared to be adding a liquid to each flask while the other was removing it. The tube that was removing the liquids emptied into a large basin that stood beside the table. There was something inside it, but Sebastian couldn't tell what it was. It had a humanistic shape, but it didn't look human. The liquid that surrounded it was the source of the yellow glow seeping underneath the door. Sebastian was too creeped out to inspect it any closer. He walked around the table and went to the back of the room. There was so much to this room. The back wall was lined in glass cabinets. He could see jars of different things in each one. He tried to open one of the cabinets, but it was locked. He made his way back towards the front of the room. In the corner, were two work stations with computers. One computer had Beatrice's picture saved as the desktop, and the other had Sebastian's. Right now, he didn't appreciate the sentiment. The desks looked unused. There were no papers of any kind found on them. The drawers of the desk were locked too. The secrecy unnerved Sebastian. What could they really be doing for the government? The desks sat back-to-back and on the wall behind them was a massive filing cabinet. He assumed it would also be locked and turned to exit the lab. He hadn't found anything out in here and knew he needed to get back to the game. As he was turning to leave, something caught his eye. The top drawer of the filing cabinet was open! He couldn't believe it. He hesitated about going over there, but knew he had to have some answers, or he would have wasted his time. This must have been what Nana was doing, because it was the only thing out of place, other than her accident. He could tell she attempted to shut the drawer, but the file got in the way, which she hadn't realized. He pulled the manila folder out. The file read, "Damion, C." There were images of a ghastly lady that started the file. She was hard to look at, Sebastian thought to himself. The next page looked like an invoice. For whatever reason, it appeared his parents had paid someone to follow this lady. There were three pages describing the vial excuse for a human being this person was. It spoke of her terrible character, her horrible lifestyle, and her crooked ways. No doubt, this was a lady Sebastian was thankful he had never had the displeasure of running into. He was angry at his parents but let out a sigh of relief that they weren't like that. As he was placing the file back, another file caught his eye. It just said Christofer. The name resonated in his mind. It seemed very familiar. He shook the feeling and began closing the cabinet. The last thing he wanted to do was read about another awful human being like the lady he had just read on. Something in his heart changed his mind. He pulled the filing cabinet back open and yanked the file out. This file was much larger, and he needed to sit down to read it. He moved over to one of the desks. He chose the one with Beatrice's photo and flicked the desk lamp on. The first page of the file was a picture of an infant. He was wrapped in a pale blue blanket and his eyes seemed very sad. He had the same color hair as Sebastian, which struck him as odd. He continued through the pages. It was a tragic story of an orphan boy. Sebastian wondered why his parents had this file of this child. He deduced it must be one of the people they were helping for the government. He had to keep reading. There were two pages dedicated to an orphanage the child was supposed to go to. It seemed like an awful place, especially for a baby. The only thing that seemed pleasant about it was the description of the yellow flowers out front. Sebastian adored yellow flowers, often he incorporated them into his paintings. They reminded him of his Mama. A twinge of pain coursed through him when he thought of her. The next page was dedicated to its caretaker. When he turned the page again, he saw one of the most beautiful ladies he had ever seen before. She had the longest hair he had ever seen, adorned with purple flowers. She was wearing a pretty purple dress. Her green eyes captivated Sebastian. He realized this must be the caretaker. There was something so familiar about her, but he knew he had never met this lady. The next page was of a very handsome man. He had a strange nose, but it seemed to suit him. The report behind his picture read of a very tragic death. Sebastian read on about how that beautiful lady in the picture experienced a downward spiral after her husband's death. Sebastian hurt for her. He turned the page again but this time he dropped the file. He knew what he saw couldn't be true. He picked it up again to make sure. There sitting in front of him, in his parent's secret lab, was a picture of his Mama. Why did they have this? Tears filled his eyes as he continued to read. He found out he was the baby in the picture. They had a file on his life. He knew he was adopted but he was angry nobody had ever shown him this file. He was also angry to find out that Ethel, he had never known her real name, wasn't really his Mama. The file didn't say where he came from and he wanted to know. There was only one page left in the file and Sebastian knew he had to read it. It may tell him where he actually came from. The last page didn't have much writing to it. The top of the page just said Ethel. So, he wasn't going to see where he came from, but he would get some more insight into the lady he thought was his Mama. The format of the page was odd. He had never seen anything like it. There were a bunch of boxes with abbreviated words in it. He continued reading. Halfway down the page, a word made Sebastian scream in terror. It couldn't be. Dead! She was dead! The file read: Deceased: Cause: Myocardial Infarction. He didn't know what the cause was, but he knew what the word deceased meant. He dropped out of the chair he was sitting in and began weeping. How could she be dead? He should have gone back to her. She may not be his actual mom, but it is who he remembered taking care of him. His mind raced to the little wooden car that was still hiding under his bed. It meant more to him now than it ever had before. He grabbed the file off the desk and opened it back up to her picture. He took the picture out and hugged it to his chest. He lay on the floor and continued crying. He wasn't holding the picture of the lady in purple, but rather the manic looking lady with the wild orange hair. This was who he remembered. He wasn't sure how long he had been crying. The tears had stopped, and he was just slowly rocking himself on the ground. It took him back to a dark time when he remembered being in a closet. He couldn't believe he had forgotten that until just now. He wanted to be angry at his Mama; but he just couldn't. He had loved her so much. Then it hit him like a ton of bricks. They knew! Mr. and Mrs. knew his

Mama had died and hadn't told him. How could they have kept that from him? Something this important should have been relayed immediately. They knew how much he loved his Mama; he was determined to go back to her all those years ago. The only thing that initially kept him there with them was Beatrice. He did wish they were in the lab today, he really wanted to give them a piece of his mind now. How could he ever forgive them for this? How could he ever look at them again? He could feel hate filling his heart. A light filled the room that interrupted his thoughts.

"What are you doing up here, child?" a voice also filled the room. It was Nana.

"Beatrice is still looking for you. I remembered I left my duster in here and was coming back to retrieve it. You are not allowed to be in here and you know that," she snapped.

Sebastian didn't move. He wanted to go run into Nana's arms and tell her everything. He wanted her to know the betrayal Mr. and Mrs. had done to him. He knew she could make the pain ease. He decided he needed her hug and slowly sat up. The most horrific thought entered his mind. He knew it couldn't be true. Not Nana. She loved the children like her own, she could never do something like this to him.

"Young man, I am talking to you, what do you have to say for yourself?" she questioned.

He stood up and slowly turned to face Nana. She gasped when she saw what he was holding. He gripped the file under his good arm. He shakily lifted the picture of his Mama up with his crippled arm. His cold stare met Nana's face. She looked down in shame. He had his answer. He wanted to hear her say it out loud. He felt his heart shatter in countless pieces. She had always been there for the children, when Mr. and Mrs. hadn't. She owed it to him to at least say it. As more hate engulfed his body, she finally looked back up at him.

"Did you know?" he managed to say unsteadily.

She dropped her eyes again, and he could see her eyes

starting to glisten with tears. He wasn't fazed.

"SAY IT," he yelled out angrily. "Did you know?"

"Yes dear, I did," she said as she began to cry.

Chapter 9: King of the Lab

Her tears didn't bother him, not now. He wondered why she had the nerve to cry in front of him. He slammed the file on the desk.

"Why didn't you say anything?" he was almost screaming at Nana.

She looked up and wiped her face with a hankie she had pulled from her apron. Sebastian had no compassion, he just stared at Nana waiting for her response. For the first time since Sebastian had come into the house, Nana was afraid of him. He had an eeriness about him she had never noticed before. His blank stare seemed lifeless. She didn't know how to answer him. She stepped closer to him and reached out her hand and placed it on his shoulder. Normally Sebastian welcomed a reassuring touch, but not this time. He shrugged her hand away. Her heart sank.

"Dear, we were just trying to do what we thought was right," she explained.

"What you thought was right?" Sebastian questioned. "In what world is it right to keep secrets like that. Did you ever think about what I would want, or was it just easier to let them sit in this dingy old file? Didn't I deserve to know the truth? Didn't I at least deserve the chance to decide if I wanted to know? I SHOULD HAVE HAD A CHOICE," he screamed as he slapped the table.

Nana jumped. She dropped her head again.

"I am sorry, dear, we did what we thought was best," she said quietly.

"Then I'll do the same," he replied coldly.

He grabbed the file off the desk and stuffed the picture back in it.

"Answer one question, and please try not to lie," Sebastian stated sarcastically. "Did Bea know?"

He held his breath as he waited for her response.

"No, dear, she doesn't know about any of it."

He exhaled. It was the answer he was hoping for and half expected. In his heart, he knew she wasn't capable of disappointing him. He began to walk towards the door.

"Leave her out of this, spare her the pain," Sebastian ordered.

Nana reached out to him one more time, but Sebastian moved away from her. He opened the door and stepped through it. He turned to shut the door, looking at Nana one last time before he left. He still couldn't believe she was a part of this. Not his Nana.

"Sebastian," she said shakily. "Did it do you any good to know that Ms. Ethel died, or to know that your biological mother was the awful Ms. Damion? We didn't see how any of that mattered for your future. We didn't want you to have that pain. We just wanted to let you start your life brand new, worry free. You had it so tough when you were young. We thought it was best," she tried to explain again.

She continued to say a few more things but Sebastian's head was spinning. He hadn't heard anything else. Had Nana just said what he thought she did? That horrible woman in the first file was his mother. His real mother. He came from her? He felt nauseous. This was too much to process. He swallowed the vomit that had formed in his mouth and shut the door, leaving a shattered Nana inside the lab. He wished he had never stepped foot in. He slowly walked down the stairs going over everything he had read about Ms. Damion. Just minutes ago, he was so thankful he hadn't ever had the displeasure of meeting her and now he knew she was his flesh and blood. He passed his sister's room and needed to see her. He picked up the pace and headed to his room. He shoved the file between his mattress and his box spring. He lay on his stomach and started fishing under his bed. He moved his good arm from left to right. Where was it? Had Nana cleaned under his bed and mistook it for trash? Panic started to set in. He needed to find it, now more than ever. He scooted closer to the headboard of the bed and finally felt the rough texture of the old wood. He pulled it out and sighed. The little wooden car his Mama had given him. One of the red wheels was now missing but he didn't care. He hugged it and felt the tears forming in his eyes again. He jumped to his feet and put the car under his pillow. He turned the light off in his room and ran down to find Bea, determined to hold it together for her once again.

He assumed she was downstairs since the light was off in her room and he had just been in his. He raced down the stairs, wiping his face as he ran. He didn't want her to know anything was wrong. He thought of their last four years together and tried to hold on to the happy memories. He filed the pain away deep into the back of his mind. As he neared the bottom of the stairs, he could see the glow of the dining room light from beneath the doors. The yellow glowing light from the lab creeped back into his mind. He shook the thought from his head again. He pushed open the doors and felt relief. There was Bea, sitting at the table eating her dinner.

"Stop right there, mister, I know exactly what you were doing," Beatrice ordered.

Sebastian froze in place. How could she possibly know? Had she followed him to the lab? Had she heard how he spoke to Nana? Had Nana come downstairs and told her everything that happened? If she had, Sebastian would definitely be speaking to Nana. He warned her to leave Beatrice out of it.

Careful not to give more information than needed, Sebastian contemplated how to respond.

"Well, don't just stand there," she continued. "What do you have to say to yourself?"

"I, um, don't know exactly how to explain it," Sebastian stuttered.

"Fine, I will do it for you," Beatrice instructed. "You decided to start our favorite game. Then you go and bend the rules by moving all over the house, so I would never actually find you. Or you found a great hiding place, still not allowing me to find you. You know how competitive I am, so you knew I wouldn't give up easily. So, I spent all that time searching for you. With all that happening, you knew it would be the exact distraction I needed to forget about what Mom and Dad had just done. You had a master plan all along, and I fell for it. I have to admit, it worked. I had a great time playing and I feel so much better. Thanks for being the best Bub ever. I know you are always trying to protect me, even if you are younger than me." Beatrice smiled and went back to her dinner.

"You are right, Bea, I am always trying to protect you," Sebastian concurred.

She chuckled and rolled her eyes. She waved him over to join her for dinner.

"You will have to get your own plate, I have no idea where Nana is," Beatrice explained.

"I told her we were going to play our game, so she told me earlier she may be turning in early tonight. She knows how our game normally goes," Sebastian instructed.

Beatrice nodded in acceptance and jumped up and ran to the kitchen. She came back within seconds with a plate of food for Sebastian. He had no appetite but was trying desperately to keep up appearances. He shot Beatrice a half-hearted smile and took a few bites. They both sat there in silence, occasionally shooting a few glances at each other. Each time they did, Sebastian felt sick. He hated keeping things from his sister, but he knew she wouldn't forgive their parents for doing this, he knew he never could. She finished her food and took their dishes to the kitchen. She announced they needed to head to bed. She ruffled his hair on her way out the door. She stopped again at the door to the dining room, told Sebastian goodnight and winked at him. This pulled at Sebastian's heart strings. She was such a great sister to him, and he was so thankful that he could always rely on her. He headed towards his room, determined to get some sleep. Emotionally, he was exhausted.

After changing into his jammies, he crawled into bed. He closed his eyes and took a deep breath. He would just process everything better in the morning. He pulled the cover to his chin and snuggled deeper into his pillow. Something poked him in his head. He remembered he had just put his toy car under the pillow. He reached to grab it. He pulled it out and held it on his chest. He ran his finger over the top of the wood. He thought back to that last year with his Mama and it was all he could take. He began to cry. He still couldn't believe she was dead. In his mind, she had moved on with her life and was happy. He had no idea how she actually died, and the uncertainty of that death saddened him. Whose fault was it? Could it have been his? He sat up on his bed and turned on his lamp. He seized the file out from his mattress and opened it. He lay the two photos of his Mama side-by-side. He was so sad that the loss of her husband had made her so manic and depressed. He never knew why his Mama had done some of the things she had to him, but after reading what she went through, it now made it easier to accept. He read the file cover to cover at least four more times. He read it until his eyes were so heavy, he was unable to open them. He fell asleep, laying on papers of his past, clutching his Mama's photos. He woke up in the middle of the night in a cold sweat. He had been dreaming about his Mama. In his dream, she was dying multiple times, each a different death. He was forced to watch each one, strapped to a chair. It was more than he could take. He had to know if there was anything else about his Mama's death. Whether he wanted to or not, he had no choice. He had to go back into that lab. He made a plan. He would go back into the lab the next night after everyone went to bed. He wanted to be more refreshed before he tried to solve any more mysteries of his past. He needed a way to put his mind at ease. He thought about the first time he met Beatrice. She was chasing that silly bunny. He smiled to himself and closed his eyes.

The next day went by in a blur. Beatrice was back to her bubbling self. They spent their entire day together. His body was present, but he didn't actually feel like he was there. He didn't see Nana at breakfast or lunch. When the kids made it into the dining hall, their food was already waiting for them. Beatrice suggested Nana must be sick or exhausted. She said it wasn't like Nana not to at least greet the children for the day. Sebastian agreed with her, although he knew she was probably trying to avoid Sebastian. He was satisfied with that decision. He really had no interest in seeing Nana either. In fact, when it was class time, he asked Beatrice to let Nana know he wasn't feeling his best and that he would be in his room resting for class. Beatrice didn't like that one bit. She stomped her feet a bit like a three-year-old. It was amusing to watch but Sebastian refused to give in.

"I know you are not sick, and you just don't want to take the History quiz," Beatrice teased.

"Trust me, I know if I go to class today, I will get very ill before the class is over. I am not quite feeling myself right now," Sebastian replied.

"Ok fine, you win. I will give Mrs. Grace the bad news. I am sure she will be just devastated," Beatrice added.

Sebastian thanked Beatrice and headed to his room. He watched as she skipped to class, none the wiser. So far, operation protect Beatrice was going as planned. He had every intention of lying down. He would need a nap before the night's adventure. First, he needed to gather a few supplies. He ran to his closet and grabbed his backpack. He thought back to the Christmas when he got it. Nana had custom designed a purple striped backpack for him. At the time, he treasured it. Nana had been so special to him. Now he looked at it, hoping to feel something similar to how he had felt that Christmas, but there was nothing. There was just an empty hole. Nana had no idea how much she had destroyed their relationship. He dumped the contents of the bag onto his closet floor. He grabbed a flashlight and threw it in the backpack. He knew he wouldn't be able to turn on the main lights of the lab, but he didn't want that creepy yellow glowing light to be the only light source he had. He grabbed a notebook of paper and pens. He wanted to document anything he felt was important. He looked behind his tennis shoes and found some gummy snacks and put them in there as well. Nana gave him a box of gummy snacks every week for him to keep in his room as his own secret stash. This was another special thing Nana had done for him over the years, that he had cherished. Why had she gone and done something that would ruin all that? He only needed one more thing. He ran to his dresser and opened the top drawer. He pulled out a red Swiss Army knife. It had gold engraving on it that read "Bud." This had been a gift from Mr. He remembered how Mr.'s face had lit up when Sebastian got it. Sebastian had never received a gift like it before. He felt grown up and proud that Mr. had trusted him with it. He now needed it to unravel the secrets they were hiding from him. Tonight was the start of the real truth. He would find out once and for all what their parents were up to and hopefully learn more about where he came from and what happened to his Mama, well, Ms. Ethel. He felt confused. He wasn't sure what to call anyone anymore. First, he needed to get some rest. He climbed into bed satisfied with his plan. With the lack of sleep from the previous night and the contentment he currently felt, it only took him seconds to fall asleep.

Hours later, he woke up screaming. He had another nightmare, but this one felt very real. It was of his ghastly mother. He hated that he even referred to her as that, chasing him in a dark alley. He was drenched in sweat again. This was the second pair of jammies he had soaked in less than 24 hours. This discovery of his past was really getting to him. His room was pitch black. It took a full minute for his eyes to adjust. It was darker than it should have been. He looked at the clock next to his bed. It was 11:30 p.m.! How did that happen? Had he really been asleep that long. Surely not. Maybe the power had gone out and his clock wasn't working correctly. He threw back the covers and ran to his window. He drew back the curtains with vigor. It was nighttime. The moon and the stars confirmed he had been asleep longer than he had originally planned. Why hadn't Beatrice woken him? He turned on his desk lamp. A soft glow revealed a note left on his desk written by his sister. He knew her writing, because she always put little hearts above her "i's".

It read, "Hey, Bub, maybe you are sick. I tried waking you and you didn't even move. Left you some food on your mantle. It may not taste very good cold. If you wake before tomorrow, come find me so we can play a game or go to our secret place. If you feel up to it. Love you. -Bea."

He never even heard her come into his room. He must have been sleepier than he realized. Well, it was too late to go to her room now. His stomach let out a growl. If it hadn't come from his own body, he would have sworn there was a lion in his room. He must have been starving. He ran to the mantel to see what was on the menu for the evening. Chicken strips, mashed potatoes, and chocolate pudding. His stomach tightened. This was one of his absolute favorite meals. He sure hoped Nana wasn't trying to win him over with food, it wouldn't work. He took his plate to his bed and began eating. The food was cold, but he didn't mind. He didn't want to risk making a lot of noise in the kitchen heating it up and Nana coming in to check to see what the noise was. So, he sat alone on his bed, eating a cold version of his favorite meal. Cold didn't affect the chocolate pudding; it was heavenly. Nana always went above and beyond in her cooking. She made a triple chocolate homemade pudding. She used dark and milk chocolate, and always put chocolate chips in it right before she served it. When the kids were well behaved, she added whipped topping and chocolate sauce. She had not done so this evening. He wondered if that was her trying to send another message. I am sorry, but it's not all my fault.

"I can't believe she is trying to act so innocent," he scoffed out loud.

He paused a moment, realizing he was complaining out loud. Annoyed by this, he grabbed his plate and returned it to the mantle. Then he grabbed his backpack and headed out of his room. He slowly opened his door and peeked out into the hall. The sconces were on, but all the rooms were dark. He was most concerned with Beatrice still being up, but there was no noise or light coming from her room. Even still, he went across the hall and put his back up against the wall. He stealthily slid down the hallway slower than most tortoises. When he came to a doorway, he eased off the wall, tiptoed sideways until he cleared the door. He did this all the way down the entire hallway. It took him nearly five minutes to make it to the end of the hall because he was moving so slow. He reached the steps that led to the lab. He contemplated just going back to his room and pretending like nothing had ever happened. He wasn't sure what else he would uncover, and he wasn't sure if he could handle much more. He remembered Beatrice's face when his parents called to say they weren't coming and felt determination sinking in. *Do it for Beatrice*, he told himself. He started ascending the staircase. He did not alternate his steps. He literally took one stair at a time as he psyched himself up to the challenge ahead. He finally made it to the lonely corridor in front of the lab. That awful yellow light was almost a caution to not enter. He shook off his nervousness and entered the code he had heard the night before. 6,4,7,2; it was clever, because although it was their birthdays, they had re-arranged the order. Beatrice, Mr., Sebastian, and then Mrs. They hadn't done it in an order that he would have ever guessed. He heard the door unlock. He turned the handle and slowly pushed the door open. He turned his head to make sure he wasn't followed. With the coast clear, he pushed the door shut, leaving him and the lab alone.

He ran to the computer where Beatrice was and turned it on. It was password protected but he figured he would just use the door code. Like he assumed, it worked. At least his parents were consistent; whether it be with passwords or their absence in the home, you could count on that consistency. He chuckled to himself at his twisted thinking. He searched through the computer and didn't find anything of value or use. His parents must be traditional when it came to keeping secrets, he deduced as he looked at the large filing cabinet. He hadn't quite built up enough courage to get any more information out of there yet. He knew that was his main mission, but he needed a few more minutes of snooping around to work up the nerve. He moved towards the back of the lab to the mysterious cabinets. He fished his swiss army knife out of his backpack. He also took his notebook and pens out and set them on the top of the counter that was on the bottom row of cabinets. He started with the first cabinet and used his knife to jimmy open the lock. He had no idea how he knew to do this, it just seemed like the right idea in his head. After just a few minutes of persistence, the cabinet opened. There were several bottles in this cabinet. Lucky for him, they are all intricately labeled. He wrote down some of the names on the bottles. Benzodiazepine, Ketamine, Propofol were among the first few he found. The names were so foreign to him. The next cabinet he opened had similar bottles in them. Haloperidol and Risperdal were among the bottles in this cabinet. He wrote all the names down and was determined to research them to see what they were used for. He began jimmying the next cabinet when he heard something in the lab. He dropped to the floor and laid on his stomach. He tried slowing his breathing and moving slowly to get behind the center table next to the glowing basin. The sound was faint, but it sounded like it was coming from the corner of the room. It was a very small squeaking sound. It almost sounded as if someone was rolling across the floor in a chair. He slowly pulled himself across the floor with his good arm, pausing to see if the location of the noise had changed. The noise had stopped all together. He slowly moved to a squatting position and duck-walked the rest of the way towards the table. The noise started again. His breathing intensified. He couldn't see all corners of the lab, so he had no idea what he was up against. He remembered his flashlight. As he was grabbing it, he quietly called out into the air.

"Nana, is that you? I have a right to the truth," he tried to say with confidence.

There was no response. He slowed to his feet. The noise had stopped again. He shakily raised his flashlight to the area he thought the noise was coming from. It was another area with bottom cabinets and a counter he hadn't seen the night before. He ran the light slowly across the cabinets. As he neared the end of the cabinets, he found the culprit of the noise. There was a small white mouse on a wheel which clearly needed to be greased. Relieved, he walked towards the mouse. There were actually three separate cages. He pulled out his notebook to document this. Each cage had a tag attached to it. Sebastian assumed were used to identify the names of the mice. He copied them down in his book. He wondered why his parents had picked such complicated names, such as: Charles Bonnett, Creutzfeldt-Jakob, and Delirium. It would have been much easier to go with names like Larry, Bob, and Chris. This partic-ular mouse was Delirium. He was running, but would stop, get off the wall and scratch at the side of the cage. Sebastian had never really been around mice, but he didn't think this behavior was appropriate. He felt bad for the mouse. He got his gummy snacks out of the front pocket of his bag. He knew it wasn't necessarily the food of choice, but he figured a mouse was probably like a dog; they would eat anything. He looked at the snacks in his head and settled on a strawberry one. He popped the treat through the cage.

"There you go, little buddy, maybe this will make you feel better," he said sweetly.

Delirium stopped scratching the side of the cage and went to the treat. He walked around three times, sniffed it, grabbed it and then ran to his little house. Satisfied that he had calmed his new friend down, Sebastian continued his exploration. He decided he would just snoop in the cabinets near the mice since he was already on that side of the lab. He jimmied open four drawers. Inside of them were syringes, gloves, needles and various medical equipment. The next drawer he pried open was very odd. There were twelve small silver devices in plastic cases. The devices had four small, sharp feet on the bottom side of them. There was a microscopic slit in the top of it. Each one had one singular button on the side. These devices were so strange, Sebastian knew he had to sketch them. In the drawer next to the cases of devices was a small black plastic box. It was the size of a deck of cards. It had one large slit on the side, and a microscopic slit on the opposite side that was exactly the same size as the silver devices. He was smart enough to know they must work jointly. However, he had no idea the significance of them or what they did. He had gathered a lot of information but knew that he would definitely need more time to figure out what all this stuff did. He had a feeling he would be spending a few more nights in the lab. He gathered all his items and put them back in his backpack. He went over to the large filing cabinet and opened the top drawer. He was ready to find out more if he could. There it was, staring him in the face again. The file on his biological mother, Mrs. C. Damion. He reached for it, he had so many unanswered questions. He graced the top of it and pulled his hand back. Just touching it made him nauseous. He couldn't do it, at least not yet. Instead, he just turned the computer and desk lamp off and retreated to the door. He left the lab and headed back down the stairs. As he reached the hallway, he heard a thud nearby. This time he didn't bother to use stealth. He sprinted as fast as he could down the hallway. He yanked open his bedroom door, dashed to his bed, without even turning off his lamp, and jumped into his bed. His heart felt like it was going to beat out of his chest. He had so much to learn. He fell asleep thinking about all the strange things he had seen in the lab.

The next couple years went by very slowly. On the surface things, for the most part, appeared to be back to normal. Sebastian was attending classes and even speaking to Mrs. Grace. He didn't go out of his way to spend time with her, and he definitely wasn't welcoming her hugs, but he was cordial to her. Mr. and Mrs. had even come home a few times over the years, and he remained cordial to them. Although he treated them this way, it was just a façade. He had grown a rage for Nana and his parents that burned inside him daily. He had found so much during his time spent in the lab. He was already angry at the adults in his life, but the things they were doing inside that lab just added to his suspicions. He tried giving Nana the cold shoulder for a couple of weeks after the initial incident, but Beatrice was picking up on it and giving him grief. He had decided he would have to put on a show to fool Nana, his parents, and sadly, even Beatrice. He didn't want her to look down on him. He felt completely justified by his feelings but knew the only way she would truly understand was if he came clean about everything. He knew he couldn't do that for two reasons. He truly was afraid that if she knew all the secrets they had kept, it would be the last straw for her too. He hated to admit it, but he was even more afraid that if she really knew where he came from, she wouldn't want to have anything to do with him either. It was too risky, she had to be left in the dark. Another day came and went, and Sebastian had started looking forward to his night escapades in the lab. He and Beatrice still played their silly games with each other and spent almost every waking moment during the day together. He was now twelve and she was fourteen. Nana had planned many play dates for them to go to, and they had played with children their own age, but they always came back to each other. There was a comfort and ease there they couldn't explain. It was an understanding of each other they had. During the day, he played the role of best bub ever. After the house grew silent, he became Sebastian, King of the lab. He had already figured out what most everything in that lab could be used for. He had taught himself how to hide all his research in a program on Mrs.' computer. He felt free in the lab. He enjoyed investigating everything inside the lab and coming up with uses and solutions for all the chemicals, medications, and devices. When his parents would come home, he had to stay out of the lab. This got under his skin. He had almost grown an addiction to the lab and his research. When they were home, after they said goodnight to the kids, he would wait up and listen. Without fail, they went to the lab. They spent their nights in the lab just like he did. The first time they went up there, he was so stressed. He wondered if they would be able to tell he was there. He wondered if he had left everything exactly the way they had. He couldn't hardly sleep that night. He kept expecting them to burst through his door, furious about him breaking the most important family rule. Nothing ever happened. They never came. He had impressed himself. He was so good and what he was doing, even his genius parents had no clue what was going on. This gave him a boost of confidence. The last time they left for work, when he snuck back up for his nightly lab adventure, he noticed that his friend, Delirium, had changed. He was now a brown mouse, instead of a white one. He wanted to know what had happened. He had looked through all their research notes in the filing cabinet and found out that they had mixed two doses of the medications he originally found in hopes to decrease hallucinations, but instead it had been lethal to poor Delirium. He felt like they were careless with this which only helped his anger for them. His parents were dealing in drugs, hallucinations, and what appeared to be mind control. He had already figured out they didn't keep all their files at this lab, which meant they probably kept them wherever they kept running off to. With missing files, Sebastian couldn't piece everything together. He still didn't know exactly what his parents were doing for the government, but he did realize it would be classified as top-secret, based off of the narcotics and equipment they had. The last mystery he needed to solve were those silver devices. He hadn't been able to find anything yet as to what they did. There was one missing from the cabinet though, so he knew whatever they were, they were currently the next project his parents were working on.

Today was like every other day for Sebastian. He spent his time with Beatrice and did all his lessons. He felt like he needed his classes. Although he wasn't keen on his teacher, he wanted to continue his education. He was determined he could be a genius just like his parents. There was no other information on Ms. Ethel, and he refused to look anymore at Ms. C. Damion. He drew the conclusion that they were a part of him. He could feel the vileness inside him sometimes. He hated the feeling but had learned to embrace it, because that is just who he was made from. She was wicked, he had wicked ideas sometimes. One couldn't blame him if that was his DNA, right? He used this idea to justify his feelings of hatred towards the people he felt most betrayed by. Ms. Ethel had told him bitterness, betrayal, and loneliness. He capitalized on this often. He hadn't felt these negative emotions in almost four years, but after what he had found out two years ago in the lab, they slowly worked his way back into his life. The only relief from this he felt anymore was when he spent time with his sister. She always reminded him of the better things in life. She reminded him of the person he wanted to be. It was an internal struggle for him. He longed for the day to end so he could get back to the lab. His focus today was strictly on those devices. It had bothered him that one was missing, and he was determined to figure out what his parents were doing with them. After he said goodnight to his sister, he waited the necessary time to head out. He had mastered this. He had to wait till about 11:00, and then, even if Bea's light was still on, he could sneak quietly enough past her room, up the stairs, and into the lab without being heard. He had a routine now. When he came to the lab, he would visit all the mice. He left each one a mouse-friendly snack in their cage. They were now all new mice and he had gotten used to this. After that, he would check on the center basin. The form in there was constantly changing size and shape. He had found logs from his parents in the filing cabinet about this research. They were trying to find a cure for cancer. They were growing a cancer mass in the basin and then using various chemicals, temperature, and light therapy to try and shrink it and ultimately stop it. Although he did feel this was very noble of them, he didn't feel it outweighed all the secrets and lies. After documenting changes to the cancer mass, he would always go to Mrs.' computer, turn on the lamp, and go over his research and discovery from his previous lab visit, especially if it had been a while before he could get back. After that, it was more snooping and research. Sometimes he even did his own experiments. Tonight's routine was planned the same. After feeding the mice, documenting changes to the mass, he went to Mrs.' computer. Before he turned the lamp on, he noticed something different in the lab. There was a faint glow coming from the other side of the computer desk. He went around to the other side and noticed Mr. had left his computer on. Not only that, but he had left a file open. This was strange, since they didn't typically use files. This must be special. The first page of the file was just a preliminary report on something his parents were referring to as "Sleep Therapy." Sebastian skimmed through it, it didn't seem to hold any significance. The next page was the blueprint for the silver devices! He couldn't believe it. The missing puzzle was right here on the computer. He thought back to the last time his parents were home. He remembered they left in the middle of the night. They had cut their trip short, again, leaving a note to their sadness of having to go. Once again, the government needed them. This time they had left a necklace and a new watch. It was the same necklace Beatrice was wearing right now. She had Sebastian put in on her. He assumed it was so he couldn't see the sadness on her face. She didn't cry anymore, which broke Sebastian's heart. She was so used to their disappointment; she had no tears left. She was loyal and selfless to a fault, though. No matter how many times they walked out on her, she always said she understood it was for the greater good. He looked down at his arm at the watch they had left. He wore it, he swore to himself it was to keep up appearances. Part of him wanted to be like his sister. He wanted to have the same type of feelings she did, but they had been buried long ago. They must have been in such a hurry; they didn't even shut the computer down properly. That was not like them. He was eager to keep reading; those devices had intrigued him from the moment he saw them. He got ready to click them again and he heard something faint. It wasn't coming from the lab, but it was coming from the house. He heard it again, this time in a set of three. What was that? It hit him like a ton of bricks. There is no way this was happening right now, not when he was about to unravel perhaps the greatest secret of the lab. If the noise was what he thought, he was in even bigger trouble. How was he going to get out of the lab unseen? He now looked down at that wrist watch, it was 11:45 at night. Why was this happening? He was sure of the sound though; it took him a second. The noise went off again, this time in a panic. He had to get out of there and fast. Who in the world was ringing the doorbell at this hour?

Chapter 10: Perfect Penny

Better yet, how was he going to get out of the lab and to his room before Nana got to the door? Nana had her own little cottage in the courtyard out the back door. However, the front door's bell system and security cameras were wired to her cottage, so she could be available at all times. She even had intercom access to the children's room in case of an emergency. By now, he assumed she had already put on her fluffy pink bathrobe and was on her way to see who was at the door. She too would be alarmed at the hour of night someone was ringing. Sebastian's room was the closest to the main entrance landing and Nana would definitely notice him running to his room and opening and closing his door. Nothing usually slid past Nana. Since he had no idea who this visitor was, he didn't know if it would require Nana to come and seek the children, which would lead her to an empty room with no Sebastian. She would then go to Beatrice's room looking for him, which would get her tangled in this mess. This was the number one thing he was trying to avoid. He needed a plan and he needed it quickly. Maybe this person would just go away. The doorbell rang again. Well, that idea had vanished as quickly as he had thought it. He grabbed his pack and headed towards the door. Hair rollers! His one saving grace. No matter what was going on, Nana would never be seen without her hair in perfect condition.

"One should always look her best, for you never know who

you will be seeing last," Sebastian said in a squeaky high voice, doing his best to imitate Nana.

He knew that Nana rolled her thin hair every night in bright pink hair rollers. It was in her routine, and she never skipped it. One time, for a week, she had the flu, spent her nights hugging the toilet, and still managed to roll her hair every night. He remembered because it was a time his parents were actually home. Beatrice and Mrs. teased Nana about it every morning when they would take her medicine and soup. It was the only time he had ever seen his parents doing things around the house because they were trying to help pick up the slack so Nana could get some rest. He never guessed in a million years he would be thankful for pink hair rollers. He got to the door and realized he may not have time to even make it to his room. In a last-minute decision, he threw his pack under his mom's computer desk and darted out of the lab. As he sprinted down the stairs, careful not to plod, he started ruffling his hair, he had to look like he just woke up. He was glad he always wore his jammies into the lab for an emergency just like this. As he reached the hallway, he could see the foyer lights turning on. The ringing of the doorbell had grown more impatient. Whoever this was, Sebastian hoped it was life or death, because this almost blew his cover. He could hear Nana grumbling, which means she was getting closer to the landing. He wasn't going to make it to his room unseen, he needed a new plan. As he was nearing Beatrice's door, he saw her light flicker on. Great, that is just what he needed. He heard the handle of her door turning, he made it to her door right as she opened it and he nearly knocked her over as she stepped out.

"Sebastian, what are you doing?" she gasped.

"I am sorry, Bea, I heard some, um, strange sound, er, I mean the doorbell, and it woke me. When I saw how late it was, I got worried and wanted to come to your room," he offered as an explanation.

It wasn't a complete lie, he tried to justify to himself.

"Well, ok scaredy cat, someone is just at the door, I am sure Nana is taking care of it. You know me though; I want to see what the fuss is all about. Let's go peek at the landing," Beatrice stated.

"Do you need me to hold your hand?" she teased as she punched Sebastian in the arm.

"Very funny," Sebastian said and rolled his eyes.

She led the way down the rest of the hallway. He couldn't believe he got away with it. It was too close for his comfort. They could now hear a very nervous voice at the door with Nana. They picked up their stride to see what was going on.

"Please, I hate to bother you at such a late hour, but I need to get back into the house and I don't know what else to do," a very large man stated.

He stood about six feet tall and was muscular in build. He was wearing teal pants and a white polo. You could see his muscles bulging from his shirt. He had the strangest facial hair. Although he didn't look very old, all his hair, both on his head and face, was white as snow. It was also very long. It was unlike anything Sebastian had ever seen. Nana seemed cautious but wasn't afraid of anyone when it came to protecting her house. She got very close to the man and stared him down.

"What did you say your name was again?" she interrogated.

"It's Tristan," he replied.

He didn't seem bothered by Nana's intensity.

"Where did you say you live?" she continued again.

"We just moved in down the road," he replied.

"Ok, come on in. You can use the phone in the kitchen. I have children asleep upstairs and we wouldn't want to wake them," Nana said quietly.

Beatrice smirked, very loudly.

"Nevermind, it seems we have company. Well come down then, dears, don't be rude," Nana ordered.

This time Sebastian punched Beatrice in the arm.

"What? She probably already knew," Bea suggested.

The kids ran down the stairs to join their new house guest. Nana told Sebastian and Beatrice to grab Mr. Tristan a fresh towel to dry off with since it had begun pouring rain and to meet them in the dining room. The kids did as they were told. By the time they had made it to the dining room with two fresh towels, it was Sebastian's idea because Mr. Tristan was a rather large man, Nana already had two cups of tea for the adults and three cups of hot cocoa. The children wondered if there would be someone else coming. After a few more moments, Mr. Tristan came back out of the kitchen and thanked Nana for her hospitality. She asked if he would like to stay and have his tea and he insisted he needed to get back. She told him to take the tea and one of the cocoas with him and just return it when he could. The kids were very confused that Nana offered to send her good china away with a stranger. She must still be half asleep! He thanked her again, said goodbye to the kids and left in a hurry.

"Well, I had just entered into a wonderful dream," Nana sighed. "Why don't we finish our drinks and head off to bed ourselves," she continued.

"Oh, Nana, aren't you going to tell us what that was all about?" Beatrice asked.

"Maybe in the morning, child, I am rather tired," Nana said.

"Oh, Nana, please, you know I won't be able to sleep if you don't," Beatrice begged, offering Nana the largest puppy dog eyes.

Sebastian knew she had her.

"Ok fine! It seems Mr. Tristan and his daughter, Penny, have moved into the house right down from us. He was working late in his study. Right before bed, he decided to take the trash out. In doing so, he locked himself out of the house. Since just his daughter and he live in the home, he takes extra safety precautions and always makes sure there are no unlocked windows or doors. His daughters' room is on the third story of the house, so he had no chance of just knocking on her window to wake her. He needed to use our phone to call the house line in an attempt to rouse her from her sleep, so she could let him in. It took several tries, but his plan finally worked. Sweet little Penny did wake up and told her Father she would wait by the front door to let him in. The whole thing is rather funny, if you ask me. However, it is too much excitement for me at this hour," Nana huffed.

At this point, Nana and both children had finished their drinks. The kids listened intently. Neither one of them had even realized there was a house near theirs, let alone anyone new moving into it. Nana was right, it had been a long night. All three were ready to retire to bed. Beatrice hugged Nana who returned the affection with a kiss on the forehead. As Sebastian passed, he could feel Bea's eyes on him, so he leaned over and gave Nana a half-hearted hug. She kissed him too. Inside, he was sickened at the gesture. He smiled and walked with Beatrice to go to bed. This was too much excitement for him as well. The pair climbed the stairs in silence, Sebastian was lost in thought. His backpack was still in the lab, but he couldn't risk getting it tonight. He prayed Nana wouldn't go in there for any reason, or even worse, his parents wouldn't make a surprise trip home tomorrow.

"Sebastian, are you listening to me?" Beatrice whined.

He didn't even realize she had been talking to him.

"Yes, of course, that sounds great," he replied, having no idea what she had actually said.

"Ok, then it's settled, we will investigate this new family tomorrow and see what we can find out. We will be like Sebastian Holmes and Beatrice Watson," she giggled.

This made him smile.

"Our own little adventure," he smirked.

"Exactly!" she exclaimed.

She hugged him goodnight, flashed her famous smile, and skipped to her room. He watched as she retreated inside and let out a long sigh. The last thing he actually wanted right now was another adventure.

Sebastian was awakened by a flood of sunlight. *Why in the world was it so bright*? he wondered. He rolled over to find the source of the light and had to immediately close his eyes because of the piercing brightness. His curtains had been drawn open. He knew he hadn't left them open, for this very reason. He chunked one of his pillows at the window. The only thing that action accomplished was knocking his lamp off his dresser.

"Good going," Beatrice teased.

This caught Sebastian off guard. He tried to stand up and without realizing it, had gotten his feet caught in his blanket and he tripped and fell on the floor next to his bed. Beatrice took this as an invitation and ran to him, hollered "pancake" and jumped on top of him. She laughed hysterically. He pushed her off of him.

"Pancake? Really Bea? We haven't done that in years," he said, annoyed.

"It's a shame really," she replied. "It is loads of fun. You should have seen your eyes while I was running to you. They were wide as saucers."

"I knew what you were going to do," he stated. "I suppose the bright and early wakeup call was your doing as well?" he questioned.

"I love how well you know me," she said as she stood, fixing her dress. "We are losing daylight. I had Nana pack our breakfast to go and told her we would be out most of the morning," she stated.

"Where are we going?" Sebastian asked.

"Our adventure. We talked about it last night. Please tell me you haven't already forgotten. Before you can say no, I won't hear it. Get up, get dressed, and let's get going. Oh, and brush your teeth, for heaven's sake," she grinned.

Her determination to accomplish things and honesty were two of the things that Sebastian adored about his sister, but this early in the morning, they were more irritating than anything else. He knew better than to argue. He untangled his feet from his blankets and slowly stood up. He turned his back to Beatrice.

"That's more like-hey, now I'll have to re-do my hair", she said mid-sentence.

Sebastian had grabbed a pillow and spun around and hit her with it.

"Good, it hadn't looked like you had done anything with it yet," he teased.

She squinted her eyes at him, stuck her tongue out, and told him to be downstairs in ten minutes. He told her he would be down in nine. She left him in the room to get ready.

Exactly ten minutes later, both children were on their bikes and driving down their long drive. Beatrice was, of course, leading the way. As she rode her bike, she would look up to the sky, close her eyes, and soak up the sun. She was so carefree. It's one of the many things he was trying to help preserve. He wished he could be that. He had almost been there before, never as free as her, but almost. He didn't feel like he could ever get that back again. They traveled another fifteen minutes before stopping at the end of a cobblestone driveway.

"Ok, this is it. I heard Nana talking to someone on the phone about where this house was. She said a gray cobblestone driveway, so I know we are here. We need to hide our bikes in the tree line and go on foot the rest of the way," Beatrice instructed.

"Why don't we just go to the front door?" Sebastian questioned.

"What kind of sleuthing is that?" she huffed while she folded her arms.

"Snooping, it is," Sebastian said, giving in. They hid their bikes and made their way up the drive using the trees as their cover. The house sat on two acres. Both sides of the entire driveway were lined with trees, which made the snooping pretty easy. Sebastian had gotten good at this over the years. As they approached the house, it wasn't like anything Sebastian had imagined. It was a three story, cream cottage with a red roof. The chimney had smoke puffing from the top. On the right side of the house was an old water wheel that was actually turning water. There was a wrought iron weather vane on top of the house with a rooster who was missing a feather. He was not expecting something that seemed so old fashioned and quaint, from a man who appeared so bold and put together. He quite enjoyed the irony. He never noticed the bounds of red hair that were flowing in the wind because he was so distracted by the house. He noticed the voice though.

"Daddy, that is the last of the boxes," she said sweetly.

He focused his attention to the source of the sound.

"Oh, she is very pretty," Bea exclaimed.

Then Sebastian saw her. There was a girl, who appeared to be Beatrice's age, walking towards the house, carrying a large box. She was wearing a long blue skirt, velvet black top, and a large bow in her hair that matched the color of her skirt. She had thin lips, a narrow nose, and piercing blue eyes. She almost appeared to be floating as she walked. Mr. Tristan was also carrying a box into the house. Sebastian had no idea what came over him, but he started walking towards the girl from the tree line.

"Get back here, Bub. What are you doing?" Bea questioned in a loud whisper.

It was too late now; he had already made it to the driveway and she had seen him. She looked a little frightened.

"Can I help you with that?" he managed to stutter.

He reached for the box and she took a step back. This angered him, he was only trying to help. Her face began to settle, and he reached for the box again.

"I am sorry about him, you know how brothers can be," Beatrice said from behind him.

She smiled a little and nodded her head.

"I don't have any, but I have friends that do," she said quietly. "I am sorry, who are you?" she asked.

"They are our neighbors, crab cake," Mr. Tristan offered as he came back out of the house.

"Dad, I told you to stop calling me that," she blushed while she handed the box to him. "I love the sea and when I was younger, I would always sneak down there anytime I got the chance. When I was about six, I snuck down and was wading in the shallows. I sat down to play in the wet sand and a crab clamped himself to my dress. I ran home crying to my dad. The crab never let go. He was very shocked when I came bursting through the door, tear-stained cheeks, and a crab attached to me. Since then he has called me that awful nickname," she explained.

"I will call you that until the day I die," Mr. Tristan jeered.

"Anyways, these are the kind folks who let me use the phone last night," he explained.

"Oh, well thank you, and it's a pleasure, my name is Penny," she sweetly said as she curtsied.

"I am Beatrice, and this is my kid brother Sebastian," Bea explained. "We live right up the road and didn't even know anybody lived nearby."

Mr. Tristan explained that their house had actually been on the market for over five years. There was not a clear reason why. Due to this, they were able to get an incredible price on it and pay for the entire home with cash. Mr. Tristan was proud of this. It allowed him to not work as many hours which gave him more time with Penny. Although it was more home than they would ever need, he had fallen in love with its charm. While they continued their conversation, Sebastian grew increasingly uncomfortable. The more they talked, the more his sister and Penny realized they had in common. They were the same age and enjoyed much of the same hobbies. They had pretty much excluded him from their conversation. Mr. Tristan had even asked Sebastian to come inside the house and give him a hand.

This did not sit well with Sebastian, but he complied. Once inside the house, Mr. Tristan had Sebastian unloading boxes of plates and putting them in a mahogany cupboard. He hadn't even wanted to come on this adventure, and now he was playing the part of obedient maid. He kept peering out the kitchen window, which overlooked the front yard, to see what the girls were doing. Every time he looked, they were laughing. He couldn't hear what they were saying, and this frustrated him. Why did Mr. Tristan think it was appropriate for him to do his housework? It didn't even seem as if Bea knew Sebastian was missing. He felt the anger bubbling in his chest. For a moment, he felt the anger directed towards his sister and that made him sick to his stomach. He needed to redirect it. This was Mr. Tristan's fault. If he hadn't asked him to come inside, he would still be with Bea and could monitor the conversation. This way, if he needed to control or re-direct it he would be able to. He needed to get back out there. He had unwrapped one box of dishes, but there were still seven more. How in the world could two people need so many dishes? He needed a way out of this task. He looked around and didn't see Mr. Tristan. He could hear cabinet doors slamming in the back bedroom and knew he must be unloading boxes back there. He peeked and saw that the girls were still caught up in their conversation. Without any hesitation, he pushed a box off the counter and onto the floor. The violent crashing of the glass dishes inside made a horrific sound. The sound echoed in Sebastian's ears. He quite liked the intensity of it. He smirked at the destruction he had just created and had to quickly wipe it away because the volume was enough for all three people who had alienated Sebastian to come running into the room. He dropped to his knees and dropped his head. Beatrice came to his side in panic.

"Bub, what happened, are you ok?" she gasped.

Pleased by her concern, he slowly looked up. Unable to lie to her, he just stared. By that time, Mr. Tristan had joined the pair on the floor.

"Sebastian, what has happened here?" he questioned.

"I am sorry, sir; my crippled arm couldn't handle the weight of the box and it slipped and fell. There wasn't anything I could do. I didn't even have time to yell for help," he falsely sulked.

"Oh, my dear boy, I am sorry I didn't even think about that when I asked you for help. Don't feel bad, this was my oversight. I will get this cleaned up, you three can go back out and play, if you wish," he kindly suggested.

Satisfied his plan worked, Sebastian slowly stood. He found it easier to manipulate the situation to his advantage than he thought it would be.

"Beatrice, I think I would just like to go home," Sebastian whimpered.

"Of course, Bub, that's a great idea," she complied. "Mr. Tristan, we are so sorry again about this. If you need anything from us, you know where to find us. Penny, it was so great to meet you. I am so happy you moved in," she gushed.

She gave Penny a quick hug. Sebastian tugged at her arm and she linked arms with him. They headed back down the driveway to retrieve their bikes, this time without using the cover of the tree line. Sebastian continued with his rouse which prompted Beatrice to spend the entire walk home attempting to make him laugh and smile. Sebastian thoroughly enjoyed the care and the attention she was giving him.

When they got home, they put their bikes back in the garage. With all the excitement, they had forgotten they had breakfast packed from Nana. Sebastian suggested they go to the courtyard and have a true picnic. Beatrice gleamed at the idea. They raced to the courtyard. Sitting near their favorite swing, they enjoyed a lovely breakfast of chocolate hazelnut croissants, fruit, and fresh squeezed orange juice. Nana had outdone herself once again. The duo laughed, joked, and took turns pushing each other on the swing.

"You know, no matter how old I get Bub, I want you to

always have enough time to push me on our swing," she gushed as she glided towards the crystal-clear sky.

"Your wish is my command," Sebastian complied.

He felt happier in that moment than he had in a long time. This was the relationship he loved between the two of them. They would always be there for each other.

"Bea, you belong to me," he said sheepishly.

"And you belong to me," she grinned in reply.

They wound up playing for two more hours outside. They opted out of lunch since they had such a late breakfast and spent their afternoon lounging in their library. They took turns reading some of their favorite stories and then they acted out a book that included dinosaurs and cavemen. Sebastian felt like the day couldn't get any better. It was now about four p.m. and they had both decided they wanted to play a game. They only had forty-five minutes before dinner, so they didn't have time for foxes and bloodhounds, so they settled for board games at the dining room table. They put up their various books and headed back towards the door. Sebastian was looking forward to continuing what had turned into a near perfect day. He hadn't even thought about the lab, his work, or his abandoned backpack that was still in the lab. As they approached the landing, Beatrice noticed Nana opening the door.

"Someone is here," she squealed as she began skipping down the stairs.

Sebastian did not share her enthusiasm. Sebastian did not rush to the door; when he finally made it, he heard Nana thanking whoever it was for returning the items so quickly. He got close enough to see the glimpse of bright red and knew exactly who was there.

"Nana, I have a grand idea," Beatrice interjected. "Couldn't Penny stay for a bit and join us for dinner? You could even invite her dad if you like, but it would be so nice of us to do."

Sebastian was dumb-founded. They had plans for the rest of their day. What did Bea think she was doing? He knew Nana wouldn't go for it. Adding two more dinner guests to Nana last minute was like trying to convince an eskimo he needed to purchase swim trunks, idiotic. Entertaining for her was a priority, and she didn't like to be frazzled with last minute planning.

"I think that is a wonderful idea, dear. I will just phone her dad and see if he would like to come," Nana agreed.

Sebastian could not believe what he just heard. The women in his house were going mad.

"Then it's settled, come on in, Penny," Beatrice invited.

"That is so kind of all of you," Penny smiled.

"Sebastian and I were about to play a game, but we have been playing all day. I am sure he wouldn't mind me showing you around instead," Beatrice said.

What was she talking about? Of course, he minded. Penny was cutting into his time.

"No, I don't mind at all. I think it's a swell idea," Sebastian coldly stated.

He was hoping Beatrice could see past the words and hear the emotion he was trying to express.

"See, told you," she triumphed.

She grabbed Penny's hand and within seconds they two were giggling all the way up the stairs. Nana had already left to call Mr. Tristan. Once again, Sebastian found himself standing all alone.

"Don't worry, I'll shut the door," he called out to an empty foyer.

He was quite annoyed by what had just transpired. Who did this Penny girl think she was? She couldn't just come into his house and take away his sister. Even though he had no real desire to speak to Nana, he longed for someone he could vent to. He kicked the front door, grunted, and turned to go to his bedroom. There was nothing else to do until dinner now.

Mr. Tristan did join them for dinner. It lasted for two hours. Everyone was in great spirits, except Sebastian. Penny gushed to her father about how incredible the mansion was. She bragged that Mr. Bunny had already taken to her, and given her bunny snuggles and kisses. This made Sebastian's stomach turn. The girls had already created a secret handshake with each other. After dinner, Mr. Tristan offered to help Nana with the dishes so the girls could spend more time with each other. He felt relieved that Penny had another female in her life, especially since her mother had left them when she was just four. Sebastian pondered how Penny could be so optimistic after finding out her mother didn't want her. He also wondered what was actually wrong with her that would cause her mom to want to leave. He intended to find out. The girls disappeared outside to the courtyard, once again leaving Sebastian. He went to his room again. He decided he would start a painting. He hadn't done that in ages. The lab had pretty much overtaken his life. He pulled his paints out and carried them to his easel. He painted in the bathroom after an incident of dripped paint all over the burgundy carpet. It had taken Nana a week to get it out and she suggested painting on the bathroom tile might be a better location. He almost painted in the middle of his room just to spite Nana but didn't want to have another incident like before and have to go through that again. As he neared the easel, he tripped and dropped a pail of red paint. The lid cracked, and red paint splattered all over his tub, toilet, and sink. He was furious. Stupid red paint and stupid red hair. He looked around at the mess and was no longer in the mood to paint. He set the rest of the paints down in the tub and turned to leave the bathroom. He didn't even want to look at it, so he shut the bathroom door. He used his intercom to find Nana and let her know that there was a huge mess in his bathroom. She agreed she would get it cleaned up once the guests left. He was offended that she didn't ask what had happened. It was almost as if she was too distracted with Mr. Tristan to even care that he had just created such a disaster. He didn't like all these changes. These two people were making huge changes in less than 24 hours. He left his room and decided he would go see what the girls were doing.

He saw that Bea's door was open and the light was on, so he went that way. When he entered the room, he didn't see them, but he could hear them. Their chuckles were coming from the closet area. Betrayal started to pour over him. Had Bea taken her to their secret place? Would she do that to him? He ran to the closet and opened the door. Both girls froze in their conversation, startled by the interruption. They were standing in Bea's closet trying on different shoes.

"Sebastian, what are you doing just barging in here like that?" Beatrice scolded.

He was embarrassed at first, but it quickly dissipated.

"Barging in? Since when is me coming into my sister's room barging in? I have always been invited," Sebastian said in rebuttal.

"Yes, but we have a guest. You need to use your manners," she snapped back.

"It's fine, I don't mind," Penny offered.

"Stay out of this," Sebastian cautioned.

The coldness in which he said it read across Penny's face.

"Sebastian! How dare you talk to her like that, get out of my room now," Beatrice ordered.

Sebastian felt the tears welling up in his eyes. His face reddened at the embarrassment of crying. He slammed the closet door and ran to his room. He jumped on his bed and began crying. He tried to control it but lost the battle. How could Beatrice act like this to him? He sat up and wiped his face again. This was not like her. It was that Penny's fault. She was changing Beatrice. She was not a good influence. He needed to warn Beatrice, talk some sense into her. He never came out of his room. Nana never came to clean and Beatrice never came to apologize for her outburst. He was distraught that they never came to check on him. He began crying again, this time softly. It was two years of pent-up tears. They didn't stop until he had passed out, emotionally drained.

When he woke up the next day, the house felt eerily quiet.

He opened his door and went into the hallway. Although it was day, it seemed dark in the hall. He didn't see any light coming from Beatrice's room. He went back into his room and called for Nana on the intercom. It took three tries, but she finally picked up. He reminded her that there was still a mess of red paint in his bathroom. She said she would take care of it after she went to the market. She needed milk, eggs, and bread. When he asked where his sister was, he was shocked by her response.

"She is at Penny's house having breakfast," she informed. "That girl hasn't eaten anywhere but here for the last fifteen years, I actually hope she is missing my French toast," Nana chuckled.

She told Sebastian she would be back in a few hours, but Mr. Tristan knew Nana was going out and she was leaving and said if Sebastian needed anything, he could call him. Sebastian rolled his eyes; he would not be contacting Mr. Tristan for anything. Sebastian wondered how he was going to spend his free time. It occurred to him he would be alone in the house. It was time to retrieve that backpack and get some lab time in. He felt a jolt of excitement course through him. He had never been in the lab in the daytime. His excitement was short-lived. Daytime lab time was just like night time lab time, except he didn't need his flashlight. He spent two hours doing more research on his parent's "dream devices." The research was fascinating. They had actually found a way to put people in short term "dream states," in which to monitor their brain activity and try to unlock the secrets of their mind. This was a voluntary experiment they were conducting. The black box and silver devices were the most important part of this process. They would use the computer and rectangle box to load a location of their choosing onto the microscopic chip. That chip was then inserted into the silver devices which were attached to the back of their neck next to the brain stem in an attempt to set the person's mind to optimum peace. Once the subject was in a dream state, it was their own subconscious that dictated the dream. His parents were attempting to find a way to manipulate and control the dream, but had been unsuccessful thus far. His dad had documented that the mind was too powerful to completely control. Most of the test subjects were reported to sleep talk while they were out. This was the desired goal, so they could get a clear picture of what the subjects were seeing. They would only keep people in the state for an hour. They had a situation that went south in the first few trials. They had put a subject under for two hours. At some point, his dream turned into more of a nightmare. Since what actually happened during the dream was determined by each test subject, there was nothing Sebastian's parents could do. At the last forty minutes of the state, he began slamming his head on the bed and began bleeding. Sebastian found this amusing. His mom had to inject him with a small dose of something called Valium to get him to relax so they could bring him out of his state. The documentation stopped there. There was nothing further on the subject and what happened to him. Sebastian sat back in his chair overwhelmed by what he had read. He could not believe his parents were working on something so dangerous and cool. He wondered if his parents had ever done this to him and Beatrice. He printed the research and stuffed it into his backpack. He needed to get out of the lab before everyone got home.

The next few months proved quite difficult for Sebastian. He was never able to find any dirt on Mr. Tristan and Penny. They were practically saints. It irked him how perfect they seemed. Beatrice also gushed almost daily about how perfect she too thought Penny was. They had grown incredibly close in a short amount of time. Beatrice had apologized for her closet outburst, although she said they shared the blame. It had been the first time he could ever remember them being at odds with each other and he hated it. They had spent the next several weeks almost as strangers in their home. Their normal jovialness was missing. Where they had spent their days joined at the hip, Penny had now become a part of that routine. She was at the house nearly every day. Sometimes they invited Sebastian, but he normally didn't have much interest. He wanted to spend time with Bea, not Penny. Every time he saw Penny, his blood boiled. In three months, he had gone from anger, to rage, then hatred. He couldn't stand anything about her. The number one thing he hated was the ability she had to monopolize and control Beatrice. If she said it, Bea did it. It was almost as if she had lost herself completely. Sebastian had tried talking to Beatrice about it, but she blew him off. She insisted he had no idea what he was talking about and was just jealous. She promised nothing had changed between them and that she still loved him dearly.

"Nobody can take your place, Bub," she had sworn.

He felt the differences though. She had once made him feel safe and loved. Most times, he just felt alone and depressed. He had no idea how to rectify the situation. He just kept hoping they would move away. Mr. Tristan had gotten a great job offer out of state, but Penny had begged him not to take it. He needed a plan, but he knew there wasn't really anything to do. Nana had come through for him, unbeknown to her, because she wouldn't allow Penny to join them for lessons. Nana said their parents wouldn't go for it. When it came to their education and their lessons, everything had to be spot on. Beatrice had teared up, given her puppy dog eyes, and begged Nana to call her parents and ask. Nana put her foot down, refusing to allow her to be persuaded. She also added that her parents had called and were on a three-month special assignment and would not have access to phone contact for the entire time. Beatrice knew there was not going to be any way to change her mind, so she reluctantly gave up trying. Sebastian relished class now more than he ever had because of his alone time with Beatrice. Although the class setting wasn't ideal, Ms. Grace didn't allow any funny business, it was still just the two of them; it brought him so much comfort. On this particular day, Ms. Grace assigned a history project to Beatrice and Sebastian. She instructed they had to work on it together. Sebastian was elated. Bea knew how much he cared about his grades; she would have to spend the adequate time with him on this. Ms. Grace suggested they should start on it right away and both children nodded in agreement. Sebastian couldn't wait for class to be over. He had everything planned. They could convince Nana to let them eat in their library and work on their project until bed. They would practically get five uninterrupted hours together. He watched the clock tick away, seconds at a time. He only had five minutes left, but to him it seemed like an eternity. As soon as class was over, he divulged his plan to Bea, and much to his pleasure, she enthusiastically agreed. Even Nana was on board with having dinner in the library. Normally she said she wouldn't be keen on it, but as long as they were working on educational matters, she couldn't argue with it. They packed their backpacks and walked out of class. They were going to drop their bags in their rooms and head straight to the library. As they neared the staircase, there were six knocks at the door. They knocked in an unusual pattern. It was two knocks in three separate groups. *"Knock-Knock, pause, Knock-Knock, pause, Knock-Knock."* Sebastian wrinkled his forehead, which caused his birth-mark to shrink in size, in confusion and Beatrice rolled her eyes.

"I know that knock anywhere," she squealed.

Sebastian felt sick. It couldn't be. Not today, they had plans today. Beatrice opened the door. It took a second for Sebastian's small chestnut eyes to adjust to the sunlight. Once they did, the sickness in his stomach increased. What was she doing here?

"Hey B, I have like an hour before my dad gets home, I wanted to see if you wanted to hang out," Penny asked.

Sebastian began to grin. He couldn't wait to see the look of rejection on poor Penny's face when his sister shot her down. They had plans and she would just have to sit this one out. Serves her right for all the times he had to miss out because of her.

"Me and Bub have a project that we need to work on," Beatrice started.

Sebastian almost laughed out loud.

"But I suppose we could start an hour later, he won't mind," she continued.

Sebastian's heart fell out of his chest. Of course, he would mind, how could she not see that? Penny. It was always Penny. Penny had already come into the house and shut the door like she owned the place. Both girls turned to Sebastian, seeking his understanding. He didn't move a muscle, nor did he respond. This time he wasn't giving in.

"Well, you know how important this project and this time is to me Bea," he coldly stated.

"One hour isn't going to make that much of a difference," Penny added.

"You're right let's go out for just an hour and then me and Bub can get to work," Beatrice agreed. "Thanks Bub, you're the absolute best," she sang as she walked past him towards the courtyard.

"Stop! Don't go with her," Sebastian blurted out. "You promised me this time, Bea. It is supposed to be the two of us," he started whimpering. At this point, the tears welled up in his eyes. "Remember, you belong to me," he pitifully said, hoping she would return their sentimental catchphrase that she began seven years ago.

"What an odd thing to say," Penny interrupted. "She doesn't belong to you? why would you say such a silly thing, Right B?" Penny questioned as she turned to Beatrice.

Beatrice's cheeks turned a deep shade of pink. She didn't really think it was weird, but she also didn't want to look odd in front of her best friend.

"Right P," she concurred.

With that, both girls headed off, hand in hand to go play. Sebastian dropped to his knees, unable to catch his breath. Beatrice had just shattered what he held most dear to his heart. The promise of him belonging to her for forever. Penny had made her ashamed of her own brother. She had finally gone too far. Penny had to go, for good. He got up from his knees in a fit of rage. He stormed to his room and started throwing anything in his sight. He grabbed his backpack to throw it and all the contents spilled out. Apparently, in his haste, he had forgotten to zip it up. This just added to the frustration. He bent over to pick up the contents and put them back in his bag. He grabbed the loose papers and saw his parents research on them. He pondered about the research again. He began to smile. Within seconds, his smile had turned into an audible laugh. It was an eerie sound that filled his entire room. This would be perfect. He would send Penny to one of his parent's "dream states." This was the perfect way to get rid of Penny. He couldn't talk sense in Bea, he couldn't make her dad move, and he couldn't kill her. Although killing her he felt was the best option, he knew it would be too messy and could be tracked back to him, so it wasn't really a feasible choice. This however could be the best answer. There were several details that had to be worked out though. The most important, he needed to figure out how to achieve "dream state" for longer than an hour. He needed it to last eternally. Unable to get into the lab, he went to his desk to start sketching out his devious plan. He knew at first, the loss of Penny would be hard on Beatrice. Ultimately, he knew she would bounce back. He was doing this for her. Penny couldn't be trusted, and he wanted to remove her from the equation now to save Bea the betrayal later.

At his desk, he started writing everything he knew from the research and what he wanted to do to improve the process. He had decided once she would be in the state, she would determine what happened in her subconscious, so he would upload the sea as her location of optimum peace. He knew she loved it as a kid, and he wasn't completely heartless. He also had to figure out where to do this. He obviously couldn't bring her to the house, because Nana cleaned every inch of the place weekly.

He also had her father to contend with. He wasn't originally thinking about it, but he was also going to have to put him into a dream state. If not, he would start a world-wide manhunt looking for his daughter. Sebastian really didn't like Mr. Tristan, but he wasn't his original target. Sebastian shrugged his shoulders. There are always casualties in war. He decided Mr. Tristan would also get the sea for his location. It would just be easier on Sebastian. Sebastian needed to get to the lab, there was so much to do. As promised, Beatrice showed back up to find Sebastian after exactly an hour. He wasn't really in the mood to do a history project anymore. He also wasn't in the mood to face his sister. She had devastated him, but he knew it was the work of Penny. She told him she was sorry. She had panicked when Penny acted the way she did about what he said. He agreed to work on the project but told her she had a lot to do to make things up to him. She ruffled his hair, pinky promised, and then hugged him tightly.

"And you belong to me," she smiled and said. "Better late than never," she added.

"Sure," Sebastian simply said.

This felt like his sister, but he knew she would never truly be herself again if Penny was still around. He had made up his mind and there was no going back.

Chapter 11: Poor Penny

He spent the next week in the lab every night for hours. He had learned that the medicine he had originally found in the cabinets were all used to put people under. He also found out that if he administered them regularly, he could keep Penny and her father under as long as he wanted. His research referred to this as a medically induced coma. He read he would need to do this through an IV, which would also double as the source he needed to give them the nutrients they would need to stay alive. He was most worried about performing this task of the process. He didn't know if he would be successful at it. He was thankful for his parent's lab. He had everything he needed at his disposal. Luckily for him, he had found that they kept an inventory sheet on their computers, so he just had to adjust the totals on their spreadsheet, so they wouldn't realize they were missing anything. They would just assume it was their own error in calculation, if they figured it out to begin with. They had such large quantities of everything he needed, he doubted it would even go missing. He had researched multiple ways on how to do the IV and had even practiced on himself several times. The first two times he did it, he nearly fainted. He had remembered a lesson Nana had taught on veins, arteries, and capillaries. He used that lesson and the knowledge he had gotten from his research to accomplish the task. By the third time, he had grown more comfortable doing it and even got a successful stick. The cold fluid dripping into his arm delighted him. It was a frigid reminder that soon, everything would be back to normal. He had also solved his problem of where to keep them. He had decided he would keep them in their own home. Knowing his sister and Nana, they would both try to contact them. He had resolved this issue too. He would write a letter to Nana for their family explaining that Mr. Tristan had taken that job. They were relocating him to a remote island where he could only communicate through two-way radios. He would explain they had to move quickly and saying goodbye in person would just be too hard on them. Since Mr. Tristan's house had been paid in full, Sebastian wouldn't have to worry about the bank coming to possess the house. He had even decided it would be best to monitor them and would use video cameras that he would link to the television in his room. His parents had bought each of them one for Christmas to record all the events they missed while they were away. They had only made one home movie before deciding to ditch the idea. Nana had spent an entire week last school year dealing with technology. She said it was rapidly evolving and the children needed to stay with the times. With every detail in place, he prepared himself for the big night. He had gone over everything at least ten times. He knew it would work; it had proven successful in his parent's research. He pondered for a second if he was going too far with things. He thought back to the instance where Penny had talked Beatrice out of saying their catchphrase. His fists tightened. His heart ached. No, he was doing exactly what was necessary to keep Beatrice to himself, to protect her in the long run. He would never hurt Beatrice, he was sure of it, but he couldn't promise the same thing from Penny. He couldn't wait any longer, tonight would be the night he would get his sister back.

As Sebastian wheeled his bike out of the side door of the garage and into the outside air, he shivered. He hadn't realized it had already gotten so cold outside. The moon was a pale yellow.

It gave off a sickly glow. There weren't many stars in the sky. The night sky seemed pathetically dull. Sebastian was relieved for the cover of the night sky; he couldn't dare to be seen. He had already preloaded everything into his backpack and was ready to do the unthinkable. He pedaled the five-mile trek to Mr. Tristan and Penny's home. It was two o'clock in the morning, he was sure he had waited long enough to ensure they were both asleep. For the first time in deciding to do this, he felt extremely nervous. Although he was a perfectionist, and he had meticulously planned every detail, there were so many things that could go wrong. He could give the wrong dose and Mr. Tristan could wake up and see him. He could give the wrong dose and kill them both. He was actually more worried about getting caught than the latter. In his heart, he knew something was wrong with that, but he didn't entertain the thought long because he had already approached the cobble-stone driveway. This time he brought his bike all the way up the hill to their house. He still ditched it into the tree line. He knew from Beatrice's lengthy detailed stories of all things Penny; they kept a secret key under a ceramic squirrel that sat on the front porch. Before he went in, he sat on the side of the house and prepared two needles with his custom mixture of Propofol and Ketamine. They were among the first drugs he found in his parent's lab. They each did similar things but were also unique to each other. Through his research, he had concluded that the two mixed together would give him almost instantaneous unconsciousness he needed. He would have to wait a mere thirty seconds, which didn't seem like long at all. He also mixed two more needles with a very small doses of SUX, which was a very dangerous drug he had also come across. He had found out that it would create paralysis of the muscles for a very small window of time, including airway muscles. Once administered, if you did not apply a breathing-tube or the antidote, the person could die. He only planned to use that if necessary. He needed a back-up plan if something didn't go right. He zipped all the needles back in his bag except his first needle for Mr. Tristan. Sebastian knew he would need to take care of him first. Sebastian took three long breaths and stood up. He unlocked the front door, slipped inside, and locked the door back. He had only been in their house two other times since the first time he met Penny, but he had an eidetic memory and knew exactly where he was going. He moved quickly and quietly to the back of the house. There was classical music playing in the living room. It calmed Sebastian. As he neared Mr. Tristan's room, he could hear him snoring loudly. If Sebastian wasn't on such a serious mission, he would have burst out laughing. It almost sounded like a freight-train crashing into a parliament of owls. His door was open, and Sebastian walked right in, closed and locked the door behind himself for privacy. He walked silently to the bed, he knew he wouldn't be able to hesitate, the longer he was in the room the more he was in danger of him waking up. The great thing about the drug mixture he made was that the needle could be stuck anywhere and be effective. Mr. Tristan's arm was exposed and closest to Sebastian. He stuck the needle in, pulled it out, and dropped to the bed and slid under it. He heard Mr. Tristan begin to rouse. "What in the world?" he began to say. The covers dropped to the floor. Sebastian began counting down from thirty. He saw Mr. Tristan's legs swing to the side of the bed, the lamp turned on from the nightstand, and then Mr. Tristan began to slide his feet into his slippers. Sebastian had just reached thirty when Mr. Tristan started to stand up. Sebastian saw him distribute the weight to stand and then to Sebastian's delight, they relaxed, and his feet went off the ground. Sebastian knew the drugs had worked; he had knocked him out. He slid out from underneath the bed and stood by him again. He checked his pulse, he had to make sure his drugs hadn't worked too well. Mr. Tristan's still had a strong pulse and regular breathing. Sebastian put a cap back on the needle and threw it back in his bag. He grabbed Mr. Tristan's legs and pushed them back into his bed. He broke a sweat doing this, he hadn't realized exactly how large Mr. Tristan actually was. He knew he should go ahead and start the IV, because he didn't want to risk the drugs wearing off and Mr. Tristan waking up. He prepared the IV. He took careful time to make sure he was doing this perfectly. To his pleasure, he was able to get him on the first stick. He tucked Mr. Tristan back into bed. With the proper drip of medications, he knew Mr. Tristan would remain unconscious. Sebastian was going to go ahead and subdue Penny before he inserted the dream state devices. He couldn't risk her walking in on the process; he wasn't completely confident he could overpower her. He checked Mr. Tristan's vitals once more before leaving. He grabbed his supplies and went back into the main part of the living room. With his first success under his belt, he felt at ease in what he was doing. He still used stealth when climbing the staircase to where Penny was sleeping. He remembered she was on the third floor. As he reached the top, there was only one door to choose. This reminded him of his parent's lab. He had uncovered so many secrets there and knew Penny's room probably had deep secrets as well. He turned the doorknob with grace and eased the door open. He was grateful that she had a lamp clicked on, it allowed just enough light for him to maneuver her room with ease. He was pleasantly surprised by the décor. Penny's entire room was decorated like the ocean. He felt like he had just stepped onto the beach, and he had never been before, but they had studied them in class. She had images of fish, crabs, and seagulls on her walls. It appeared as if she had personally done them. They weren't too bad; he wouldn't recommend hanging them in any gallery, but still they were nice to look at. There was a very large seashell collection on top of a very wide dresser. He knew he had made the right decision with their dreamscape location. She was asleep on her side, with her back facing the side of the bed Sebastian was creeping too. He lay on the floor next to her bed, unzipped his back and grabbed the second "sleeping" needle. As he slowly rose to his knees to stick her, he almost gasped out loud. She had rolled over and he was now face to face with her. Unsure if she was waking, he tried to lay back down but couldn't move. He was frozen in fear. Her breathing was steady, and she wasn't moving so he deduced she was still sleeping. His eyes had completely adjusted to the room and he could finally tell that her eyes were closed. He watched her sleep for a moment. She really was very pretty, although he had never actually wanted to admit it. He couldn't believe someone so pretty could cause so much ugly destruction. He worked his nerve back up and stuck the needle in her shoulder, pulled it out, and laid back down beside the bed. He attempted to roll under it, but it was solid to the floor and lined with drawers. This made him nervous because he had nowhere to hide. He began counting again, just like he had done in her Father's room. When he had finished counting, he slowly peered up over the edge of the bed. Penny was in the exact same position as before. It didn't seem as if she had even moved an inch. He wondered if it had worked. He needed to know before he started an IV. With her dad, it was easy to tell, he literally fell down unconscious in the middle of trying to stand. With not many options he whispered her name.

"Penny, Penny, are you awake?"

There was no response. He bit his lip trying to think of what else he could to test it. He grabbed her arm, lifted it into the air, and dropped it. It was limp like spaghetti and she still didn't move. He was satisfied it had worked and he felt a sense of relief flood over him. He also checked her vitals. She was still alive.

"Yay," he sarcastically whispered.

He went to the main light of her room and clicked it on. He rolled her to her back and began the IV process. He moved much quicker than he did with her Father. As he continued working, he began thinking about everything he had just accomplished. He was just a stupid little orphan boy that nobody wanted and look at him now. He had been given up twice in his life, and although he had parents now, they didn't seem to love him enough to ever be present. He was very smart and had just pulled off exactly what his parents were doing for the government. That had to make it at least a little special, right? He spent the next thirty minutes setting up the cameras in the house. All that was left were the dream devices. He started by adjusting the fluid in their IV bags. He needed to add a mix of hallucinogenic drugs to the bag, so they could stay trapped inside their dream and have no way to associate with reality. This would increase their chance of altered sleep. All that was left were his little silver bullets. His parents just referred to them as devices, but he knew they needed a catchy name if he was going to be working with them. He had already loaded the microscopic chip with the sea scene. All he had to do was insert them and push the button to turn them on. The mix of drugs and their mind would do the rest. He tilted Mr. Tristan's head and pushed the bullet into the back of his neck with force. Thin lines of blood seeped from his neck, which caught Sebastian off guard. That wasn't anywhere in his research, but he supposed he should have expected it. He grabbed some toilet paper from the bathroom and wiped it up. The coppery smell of the blood turned his stomach a little. He pushed the small button to power it on, and then flushed the toilet paper, careful not to leave any evidence of his being there. He then went to Penny's room to follow the same steps. After he was finished, he sat down on her bed and watched her sleep. He wondered if he would start talking just like her parent's test subjects. He sat and watched her sleep for about fifteen minutes. He still had things he needed to do, so he couldn't wait any longer. He turned all the lights off in her room and headed out the door. As he was leaving, she faintly said, "There is water everywhere," but Sebastian never heard her. He went through the house and turned off all signs of life. He even disconnected the landlines. He knew his sister, and she would march right to the house and pound on the door. Satisfied the house looked empty on the inside, he went outside. He pulled Penny's bike and all their yard ornaments into the garage. He disabled the garage door, so he couldn't be opened with a device. He was pleased they didn't have a window in the garage door because his sister would find a way to peek in. He went back to his bike and pulled something off that he was quite impressed by. He couldn't believe he had thought about it. He had painted a very professional looking "for sale" sign. He found some old wood and tools in Mr. Tristan's garage. He attached the sign to the wood post and drove it into the ground. It took him longer than expected because of his crippled arm, which infuriated him. The night sky had dissipated, and he could tell the day sky was waking. He had to hurry, Nana was always up and moving between 7:00 am and 7:30 am. His watch read 6:30 am. He had to hustle. He stepped back to look at the house. It looked completely deserted. He zipped the key in his backpack, picked his bike up, and headed towards his house. He triumphed all the way home. Although it was only a fifteen-minute ride, he pedaled as fast as he could. He didn't want to risk being seen by anyone traveling. He had planned to be home by 5:00 am, but it took him longer than anticipated to accomplish everything. He made it home in ten minutes and was completely out of breath. He dropped his bike outside the garage and decided to enter through the front door. It was less risky, because it had a direct route to his room. His hands were shaking as he rummaged through his bag to find his house keys and unlock the door. He knew he was running out of time, if Nana decided to wake early, his goose was cooked. He sprinted to his room and changed into his jammies. He had to quickly hide the evidence of everything that had just happened. He was disappointed he wouldn't be able to check in on his new projects. He smiled at the idea of being in control of them. He ran to his closet and pushed his pants to one side. His parents had given him a hope chest for his 8th birthday. They explained the sentiment, which he still didn't understand, but was grateful he had it now. Nana had already put things in there, including a quilt she had made for him that she said he could put on his marriage bed. He never intended on getting married, so he never intended on using it. He pulled it out, put his backpack in the chest, and covered it with the quilt. Even if Nana added something to the chest, she wouldn't move the quilt to do so. It was perhaps the one place in his room that everything would be safe in. He fixed his pants, shut his closet door, and jumped into bed. He checked his watch, 7:00. He had just made it. He thought he may need to actually get some sleep. He closed his eyes and let out a long breath, pure satisfaction. Within seconds he shot up in the bed. The letter! He had forgotten to write the letter at their house and leave it on the door, where he knew his sister would find it eventually. This was the most crucial step of the deception part of his plan. He threw his covers off and ran to his desk. This had to be perfect, or the whole thing would be ruined. He grabbed a piece of paper and a red pen. He knew he needed to write in a unique color and writing or Ms. Grace would see right past it. He didn't know how to conceal his writing. He really hadn't thought this through very well and he began to panic. How was he going to cover his writing? Why hadn't he thought this through better? His arm, his crippled arm. For the first time in his life he was thankful for such an inconvenience. He had never tried writing with it, so Ms. Grace would have nothing to compare it to. It was perfect. He began the letter, he wanted to keep it short and sweet.

"Dear Nana, Beatrice, and little Sebastian,

It is with heavy hearts and great sadness that we write to you. I have decided it is best for me to take that job, however they have decided to move me even further away than I originally knew. I know it won't make sense to any of you, and it will be hard to leave my house, but it is the best thing for my daughter and me. Please do not try to contact us, because it will be to no avail. Where we are going, there is no communication, except through two-way radios. I have put my beloved home up for sale, and I have a distant relative who will be looking over all my affairs. We have already left; goodbyes would have been more than Penny could bear. She asked for me to also write for her to Beatrice. You were the best friend a girl could ask for you. You are such a wonderful person, and anyone would be lucky to have you in their life. I didn't deserve a friend like you. I wasn't worthy enough. I will always remember you, B. Love, P."

Satisfied the letter would do the trick he put it with his backpack. He would have to get back to their house somehow and stick it on their door. This was an unfortunate oversight, but he would just have to make it work. He checked his watch again, 7:29 am, just in time to sneak back to bed for a little bit. He climbed back into bed, pulled the covers to his chin and closed his eyes. Within seconds, his door sprang open.

"Rise and shine, Bub," Beatrice sang.

Sebastian groaned internally. What on earth was she doing in his room so early? As if she was reading his mind, she responded.

"Nana woke me on the intercom to let me know breakfast would be an hour early today because we have an extra-long class session today because of our project. So, we have to be downstairs in thirty minutes. I offered to come wake you myself."

By this time, she was bouncing on his bed. He tried to remain calm, but his night had instantly caught up with him and he was exhausted.

"I don't feel well, I don't think I can go to class today," Sebastian muttered.

"Oh no, you don't! You are not getting off like that, and sticking me to do this project by myself," Beatrice pouted.

She pulled the covers off of him and started rolling him off his bed. Right before he reached the edge, he told her to stop, that he was getting up. She grinned at her victory. She told him she needed to go get changed and would be back in his room at 7:55 am. He gave her a weak thumbs up and collapsed back onto his bed. How was he going to focus on class without even getting a nap? He decided to shower to help revive himself, and even contemplated drinking coffee for the first time. This was going to be a very long day indeed.

After he was dressed and ready, he and Bea walked to breakfast together. She was in such a great mood and he wished he could match her spirit. He was relieved Beatrice was so talkative at breakfast because he was able to smile, nod his head, and every once in a while, grunt in agreement and she was completely pleased by their transaction. It didn't require much brain power, and he was thankful for that. After breakfast, they went to class. This was going to be harder to get through than breakfast was. Over the next five hours, Sebastian fell asleep at least twenty times. One of them was so bad, he even fell out of his chair. That one resulted in him needing to write "I will not fall asleep in Ms.' Grace's class ever again. I will make sure to get plenty of sleep the night before" 100 times before the next class. Ms. Grace really didn't tolerate shenanigans in her classroom. He was too tired to be angry at the assignment. When class was finally over, Sebastian just wanted to sleep. Beatrice had asked him if he wanted to play in the courtyard, and as much as he wanted to say yes, he just couldn't. His body wouldn't allow it. He declined and told her he needed to lay down. She teased him for a bit but ultimately told him she thought it was a great idea because he looked awful. As he was making his way to the staircase, he heard Bea calling for Nana. As he neared the landing, he heard something that stopped him dead in his tracks.

"Yes dear, you could go see Penny, I don't mind," Nana replied.

Sebastian's heart sank. No, she couldn't go do that, he hadn't had a chance to place the letter. He needed to think fast, but his brain was not working.

"Nana, Nana, Nana" he practically screamed over the landing.

Nana and Beatrice both came running to the staircase.

"What is wrong, dear?" Nana questioned in a panic. "Is everything all right?"

"Yes, I just, um-I am out of shampoo and soap. I need some more, like today," Sebastian lied.

He shook his head at his own stupidity. That was the best he could do. It wasn't enough to involve Beatrice, yet.

"But I want new scents, I don't like the old ones. I don't know what would be best though, so someone is going to have to pick them out for me," he continued.

"I'll do it, oh please, Bub, let me pick the new ones," Beatrice pleaded.

He knew that would get her. She was always trying to style him and help him improve. She said it was a sister's job to make her little brother look and smell the best he could.

"Well, I guess there are a few other things I could stand to get for the house," Nana pondered out loud. "Yes, we can go to town now and get it, would you like to come?" Nana asked.

"No ma'am, I really do need to take a nap and work on my sentences," Sebastian offered.

"That is very true, but don't be late for dinner," Nana replied.

"You got it," Sebastian said with a forced smile.

Nana was a little caught off guard by his politeness. She hadn't seen that in some time.

"I got shot-gun," Beatrice teased.

"You are a silly girl," Nana said as she patted her on the back.

Sebastian watched as both ladies left the house. He went back down the stairs and to the window. He saw the car pull out of the garage and head down the driveway. Although it was a last-minute idea, it actually was a perfect one. They would need to take a right to go to town, and Penny's house was to the left. He could leave right now and go deliver the letter and not worry about running into them. Since it took thirty minutes to get to town, he knew he had plenty of time. The only thing he was worried about was his body not making it.

He had made it to their house, put the letter on the front door, and made it back within thirty minutes. He knew Nana and Bea would have just made it to town. He was elated. He literally had no energy left as he made it to his bed and plopped down. He didn't even bother taking his shoes off or getting under the covers. He had only been asleep for three hours when Beatrice burst into his room, startling him awake. *She really needed to work on this,* he thought to himself. It had gotten dark in his room and his eyes hadn't adjusted to her yet. He could hear her though, and she was weeping. She climbed into his bed and lay down next to him.

"How could she do this to me?" Beatrice sobbed.

It took him a second to realize what was going on. Finally, he understood she must have found the letter. He was glad he delivered it when he did because she had not wasted any time. He was wide awake now.

"Who are you talking about?" he questioned innocently.

"Penny," she whined. "She is gone. She just left. Her dad took that stupid job she had begged him not to. It doesn't make sense. She didn't even come to see me to say goodbye. Nana and I went to the house. It is completely empty. There is no trace of them at all."

Sebastian was glad his room was dark, because he could not contain his wide-crooked smile. He had completely pulled it off. He had fooled everyone. He had to stop gloating. His sister needed him right now, and he knew this would happen. He began patting her on the back.

"Shush, don't cry," he coddled. "You are far too pretty to cry. You wouldn't have been able to say goodbye to her in person either. If Mr. Tristan left that house, you know he must have had a really good reason."

"Maybe you are right," she sniffled.

"Besides, she wasn't that great, ya know," he continued.

"What are you talking about, she was the best," Beatrice

moaned.

He knew he had gone too far with his personal opinions.

"I meant she wasn't as great as you, I mean nobody is," he flattered.

"Ok, I see what you are doing. Flattery isn't going to work while I'm so sad," she instructed.

"You think I'm the greatest?" she sweetly asked.

He knew it was working.

"In the whole world," he said as he hugged her. "You want to play a game or something?" he asked, trying to distract.

"Actually, not really," she replied. "I do feel a tad better, but I just need some time to process everything ok. I will be fine," she promised.

Sebastian told her he understood. Bea said she didn't want dinner this evening. Sebastian assured he would tell Nana. Beatrice hugged him again and headed to her room for the evening. It did hurt him to see her in such pain, but he knew it would pass, and knew he was saving her from a world of hurt in the future. If nobody ever got close to her, nobody could ever hurt her. He would always protect her.

He kept true to his word. He went and found Nana. She hadn't started dinner yet. She told Sebastian she was waiting on his nap to be over, so he wouldn't miss dinner. He told Nana that he and Beatrice were just too upset about the whole Penny situation to have a formal family dinner.

"Really, you didn't seem too keen on her, Sebastian," Nana replied.

"I hide my emotions well," he stated.

He was not about to let Nana turn this situation around on him. He didn't wait for a rebuttal. He just turned and ran out of the kitchen. He had things he needed to do. Once he was in his room, he locked his door. Beatrice had gotten really good at barging in and he didn't need that to happen right now. He went to his tv and turned it on. He changed the input and found the necessary feed that had Penny and her father on them. There they were. The video was a bit blurred, but he could see and hear everything he needed to. He grabbed his notebook from his backpack and a chair. He sat down with a pen and prepared himself to write.

Meanwhile in Penny's room, it was a shame that such a young girl's life was pretty much over. Penny woke to find herself on a beach.

"Where am I?" she wondered out loud.

She could smell the fish in the air. She could taste the salt on her tongue. It looked just like the beach she was at when she was little.

"How did I get here?" she contemplated.

She took a step forward and felt the wet sand squish in between her toes. She loved that feeling. She still didn't have any idea how she had gotten to this beach; she began looking around. The place was deserted. When she was younger, this same beach was riddled with people. She wondered where they were now. In the far distance, she could see someone laying down. She was frightened and didn't want to go near them. She assumed her dad had gone to get food or get something out of the car. She felt a chill as the wind blew. She looked down and gasped. What was she wearing? She had a purple swimsuit top and a teal swim skirt on. She would never mix these colors. Better yet, how did she get it on? She began to feel herself hyperventilating. She put her hands on her head, to control her breathing. Her face twisted in more confusion. She ran her left hand down the length of her hair. A braid? Her hair was braided and had tiny seashells in it. She only ever wore her hair down. What on earth was going on? Maybe she had fallen asleep in the car and didn't remember getting here. Maybe she had gotten heat stroke and that's why she couldn't remember. She was not good with medical stuff, so she just shook the thoughts out of her head and tried to enjoy herself. She walked towards the water; it looked very inviting. She got about knee deep and started freaking out. She couldn't move her feet or legs. They were stuck together, and she had no idea why. She screamed in panic and fell down. She pulled herself out of the water with her arms. As soon as she reached the bank, she regained control of her legs. Just then, a seagull flew and squawked overhead. Penny knew she was losing her mind, it almost sounded as if it said hello. She pulled her knees to her chest and wrapped her arms around them. She was totally freaked. She lay her head down and began sobbing. She stayed that way for five minutes.

"Why are you crying?" a tiny voice asked.

She looked up and saw a yellow and blue fish, and a marron crab looking at her. They were sitting in the shallowest part of the water staring at her. She just stared; it wasn't possible. They stared back. She scooted further away from the water and began sobbing.

Tristan woke up to a gush of water engulfing his body. He rolled over and began coughing. His eyes burned from the salt. It took him a second to fully process that he was awake.

Am I dreaming, he thought to himself.

He pinched his left arm and let out a small squeal. Definitely not a dream, the red mark on his arm proved it.

"Acitnalta Beach," he stammered. "How did I get here? We haven't been in here in like ten years. Did we have an accident?"

He looked around trying to find a car or boat, or anything to explain him washed up on the shore. Panic set in. Where was Penny? Mr. Tristan was an overly protective father and needed to know where his daughter was at all times. He needed to find her. He stood up and looked around. The sun was blazing. He had to cup his hands over his eyes. He saw her. Far off in the distance, he saw bright red. He knew that shade anywhere. It was his pride and joy. How had she gotten so far from him? He needed to go to her. She was sitting down, but he couldn't tell what she was doing. He began to run to her. He got about fifty feet and was knocked to his backside. He got up and tried again with the same result. He had no idea why this was happening.

He went to the same location, but he kept getting knocked back and slowly lifted his hand. There was some type of invisible barrier.

"This isn't even possible," he grumbled.

He needed to use something other than his body to try and get through. He went back to where he was laying. He noticed some driftwood near the beach. He went to the shallows and started rummaging through it. He found the perfect piece. It was as long as he was tall and had a pitchfork shape on the top of it. He went back to the barrier and tried jarring his new weapon into it. It didn't work, but he was not going to give up. He had to rescue Penny.

Sebastian watched Penny and Mr. Tristan on the feed. Their bodies appeared lifeless. He actually thought maybe he could start appreciating Penny, especially if this is how she would stay. He chuckled to himself. He had been monitoring them for over an hour. He looked down at his notes.

"Mr. Tristan-Penny, barrier, stick". Those were the things he had said. "Penny-clothes, bird, fish, crab, and scared." Those were the things she had said. He had no idea what any of it meant, but he knew his little bullets were working. He would have to make a daily visit to their home to restock their meds and nutrients. They were good until tonight. He closed his notebook, changed the input back on his tv, and shut it off. He went back to his closet and put his things in his new secret hiding place.

"Sebastian, you are a genius," he gloated to himself.

Everything was in order. He sat down and wrote a lovely note to his sister, trying again to lift his spirits. He exited his room and slid the note under her door. He was so elated that things were working out so well, he skipped back to his room. Everything was perfect. He changed into his jammies, shut his light off, and crawled into bed. For the first time in a long time, he knew he would sleep like a kitten. He smiled as he thought about Penny's last word on his notepad.

"Serves you right to be scared. You wanted to be in my world, you got it," he snarled.

Things you probably don't know...

I am a foster momma with six kiddos. They are ages 3-8 and they are all so different. When we go places, people like to ask me if we are a Sunday School or Field Trip group-NOPE, just my family.

I married the boy I have loved since I was 16. He is now a travel nurse and was a COVID nurse when things were super scary, and I am just thankful he stayed healthy.

I previously worked as a 911 dispatcher/hostage negotiator, turned Christian School Principal (Same training), and now I get to SAHM and work as a social media manager, book coach, public speaker, and am diving deep into my dream of being a published author.

We also breed Bernedoodles, raise chickens and goats, and enjoy every breath God has given us.

I am able to do all this by the love and support of family, friends, and running on Jesus & Coffee!

This is the scariest and most challenging thing I have ever done but with every new reader I meet, I am living my dream!

I hope you enjoy my books & join my newsletter: http://www.authorsavyloy.com

ReSet: Be Good, Your Life Depends on it

ReBorn: Second Chances

BeeBerry: A Lesson in O-Bee-Dience